'It's not a problem, is it?'

'Problem?' Swinging around for the first time, she managed to actually look at him, her eyes frowning as they met his.

'Me.' Rory looked back at her. 'Being here. If it is you just have to say. I don't want to…' For a second he faltered. 'I mean, if your boyfriend's going to be worried by my staying here then you just have to say.'

'Why would it be a problem, Rory?' Still she looked at him, even managed a very thin smile. 'I've got an old friend staying for a couple of weeks until he finds somewhere else. Why would anyone have a *problem* with that?' Walking to her car, thankful the door was unlocked, Ally slid inside. Shaking hands pushed the key in the ignition, then she attempted a smart reverse, miserably failing, instead doing bunny hops the whole length of her driveway.

She'd sit in the movies alone if she had to!

Watch the same film twice over if it kept her out till after midnight.

Anything other than let him glimpse the effect his return was having on her.

Carol Marinelli recently filled in a form where she was asked for her job title, and was thrilled, after all these years, to be able to put down her answer as writer. Then it asked what Carol did for relaxation, and after chewing her pen for a moment, she put down the truth—writing. The third question asked: What are your hobbies? Well, not wanting to look obsessed or, worse still, boring, she crossed the fingers on her free hand and answered swimming and tennis. But, given that the chlorine in the pool does terrible things to her highlights, and the closest she's got to a tennis racket in the last couple of years is watching the Australian Open—I'm sure you can guess the real answer!

Recent titles by the same author:

NEEDED: FULL-TIME FATHER
CHRISTMAS ON THE CHILDREN'S WARD
SPANISH DOCTOR, PREGNANT NURSE
  (Mediterranean Doctors)
UNDERCOVER AT CITY HOSPITAL
  (Police Surgeons)

THE MIDWIFE'S SPECIAL DELIVERY

BY
CAROL MARINELLI

MILLS & BOON®

First published in Great Britain 2006
Large Print edition 2007
Harlequin Mills & Boon Limited,
Eton House, 18-24 Paradise Road,
Richmond, Surrey TW9 1SR

© Carol Marinelli 2006

ISBN-13: 978 0 263 19331 2
ISBN-10:   0 263 19331 4

Set in Times Roman 17¼ on 20½ pt.
17-0107-45892

Printed and bound in Great Britain
by Antony Rowe Ltd, Chippenham, Wiltshire

PROLOGUE

'HEY!'

Gripping the phone receiver in her hand, Ally Jameson closed her eyes as the call she had been both half expecting and half dreading came when—as all her horoscopes had said it would—she was least expecting it.

Well, not quite.

Since she'd heard that the new registrar starting on Monday at Bay View Hospital was none other than Rory Donovan, she'd been wondering if, after three years, he'd ring and say hi.

Or 'hey'.

So far tonight she'd had the two *very* un-Australian voices bidding her 'g'day' and telling her they could solve all her financial woes if she would only fill in a quick survey; one lovely lady telling her that if she wanted to leave her unwanted clothing and furniture on the nature strip on Monday, she would send someone to pick it up; and a rather irate gentleman demanding to know why she didn't want to subscribe to the fabulous once-in-a-lifetime gym subscription he was offering.

Tired, ratty and horribly fed up, Ally had put on a face pack and painted her toenails scarlet, poured a glass of wine and convinced herself she was a fool for even thinking Rory would ring to tell her he was coming back to Bay Side. After all, why would he? They'd only shared a house for a few years, shared the same social group. In their time together they'd been nothing more than friends, hadn't even dated.

And then the phone had rung.

For a second Ally wondered if it would be rather more dignified to pretend she had no idea who was calling, to pretend, after all these years, to have no idea who the voice on the other end of the phone belonged to.

'Hey!' Face pack crumbling as quickly as her resolve, Ally's face broke into a wistful smile. 'Long time no hear.'

'I know.' A lot of muffled background noise ensued and Ally frowned into the phone.

'Where are you?'

'At the airport—not Melbourne airport,' he added quickly, the phone line crackling as if it had been dipped in hot oil. 'So don't worry, I'm not ringing to ask for a lift.'

'Makes a change.' Ally smiled, shouting to be heard. 'Where are you, then?'

'Bali…' The line crackled again. 'End of season footy trip. I get in tomorrow. Did you hear the news? I'm coming back…'

'You start Monday!' Ally broke in when the line crackled yet again. 'I heard. Congratulations, Rory.'

'Any chance of renting a room from my old landlady?'

And the silence this time had nothing to do with the appalling line, nothing to do with the fact he was at a call box in Bali, and everything to do with the fact she hadn't seen him for three years. Everything to do with the fact that the last time she'd seen him, he'd literally broken her heart.

'Look, no drama if I can't,' Rory carried on, clearly oblivious to the turmoil he'd created. 'I've got a room at the doctors' mess. I just thought I'd ask…'

'I don't take tenants any more,' Ally said, then instantly regretted her rather prim tone— as if those years of laughter, parties and fun had been to do with money. 'I mean, you'd be horribly bored, it's nothing like it was— there's just me here now. I don't need the rent or anything.' She was blabbering now, horribly so, trying to sound casual and somehow trying to keep him at arm's length.

'If it makes it easier for you, I won't pay rent!' He started to laugh, and it sounded the same as she remembered, so much so that Ally closed her eyes, pictured that smile on his face, his laid-back humour, his take-it-or-leave-it jokes, and could scarcely believe that after all this time she was talking to him. That Rory was on the other end of the phone, asking to move back in. Rory would be working with her from Monday. 'Don't worry about it.' She could hear the pips going on the phone, knew that his money was running out. That ever sensible part of her brain was telling her to just let it go, let his money run out, let him hang up—the same way he'd hung up on them all those years ago.

So why was she shouting into the phone?

'Sure—no drama. If I'm at work when you get here, the key's still in the same place!'

'You don't mind?' Rory checked. 'It's just for a couple of weeks until I…'

His money must have run out, or maybe, Ally thought as she hung up, Rory Donovan had got what he wanted, sorted out his accommodation and moved on to something more important: his footy mates and a glass of beer.

'That was Rory!' Ally said, staring into the somber, cloudy eyes of Sheba—the oldest, smelliest Labrador in Australia. 'It sounds like he's coming home.'

Home?

There wasn't much of her face pack left to peel off but, unnerved now, Ally headed to the bathroom and rinsed off the remains and brushed her teeth, before finally lifting her face and staring in the mirror, trying to envisage somehow what Rory would see.

The dark short curls were long now, way past her shoulders, which sounded far better than it looked, Ally decided, holding up the rather frizzy ends and vowing to book herself in for a very overdue trim.

Her skin had cleared up at least.

Thanks to an appallingly delayed adolescence, the last time he'd seen her she'd had a T-zone you could drive a car down. She'd been sure that she'd end her days in a nursing home and, instead of a glass jar for her teeth, she'd have a bottle of acne lotion by her bed, but at twenty-seven years of age her skin was finally, after the longest time, spot-free. Her eyes were still boringly brown, of course, and her lashes, despite nightly rubbing with Vaseline and the most expensive eyelash curler, were still short and spiky.

Not that he'd notice.

Not that he'd ever noticed.

Except for once. Firmly pushing that thought out of her mind, Ally peeled off her T-shirt and, pulling on a bigger, baggier one, crawled into bed. Reaching for the alarm clock, she wondered if she should set it, tried to work out the flying hours from Bali to Melbourne and gave up.

She damn well wasn't going to be standing at the door welcoming him and she sure as hell wasn't about to put clean sheets on the spare bed and make a mad dash to the bakery for rolls.

He could take her as he found her.

Twenty-seven years old with a beautiful home, a great career and a fabulous group of friends.

Rory Donovan could take her as he found her…

Instead of where he'd left her…

CHAPTER ONE

So MUCH for fresh rolls!

Pulling on her uniform, Ally cut off a piece of cheese and rammed it into the offending article, furious with herself that despite her stern promises she'd awoken at the crack of dawn and headed straight for the baker's, furious with herself that she'd made up Rory's bed and put on some coffee, not to mention five hundred coats of mascara—furious because she'd expected more from herself.

It was midday!

Midday and, even allowing for delays, even allowing for customs and a massive queue at the taxi rank he should have been here hours ago.

Well, what had she expected?

Exactly what Rory had expected, Ally realised.

To walk straight back in to the accommodating, friendly girl he'd so easily said goodbye to.

Well, she wasn't that girl any more.

Throwing the jug of coffee down the sink didn't really help, but a full carton of milk and the remains of the sugar did—picturing his face when he went to make his regular, disgustingly strong, disgustingly sweet brew, he could damn well walk to the grocer's. Ripping the sheets off his freshly made-up bed, Ally shoved them in the washing machine and turned it on the longest, hottest wash the dial could summon, writing a massive note in black text and leaving it on the kitchen bench.

Sheets in the machine
Feel free to use the dryer
Ally

Not that that would stop him, Ally realised—knowing Rory, he'd either crash on the bare mattress or deviate straight to her room!

A mischievous smile played on her lips.

Heading to her bedroom, she rummaged through her knickers drawer, rummaged right to the very bottom where a pair of leopardskin knickers and bra lay—courtesy of a hen night party—still in their Cellophane. No doubt they'd crumble to dust once she opened them, but in an act of defiance Ally ripped open the pack, slung the two triangles that called themselves a bra over the chair in her bedroom and threw the G-string on the floor.

If only she had a packet of condoms to leave by the bed.

Instead, she exchanged her midwifery manual for a steamy romance she'd been meaning to read, sprayed half a bottle of perfume to scent the room, hid all her acne creams, razors and hard-skin removers and closed the door on the temporary brothel she'd created, feeling great, in control, on top of things…

Until she heard the unmistakable purr of a taxi.

Until she heard that deep, throaty voice, laughing and chatting with the driver.

Standing far back enough from her window so that she could see and hopefully be seen, Ally stared as three long years were erased in a single moment.

In an effort to keep going, in an effort to just keep breathing some days, Ally had managed to convince herself that the images that played over and over in her mind didn't actually match the reality—that if ever Rory Donovan stepped back into her life she'd be hard pushed not to throw her head back and laugh at the thought he'd once affected her so much. Had convinced herself that he wasn't really that good-looking, that loud, that big… That six feet seven could somehow shrink into normal-sized proportions!

Rory was huge—and that wasn't just according to Ally. Everyone—*everyone*—commented on his size, because Rory was a generous touch more than the average tall guy—he literally towered over everyone. He looked more like a rugby player than a doctor—minus the cauliflower ears and broken nose, though, Ally conceded, watching as he pulled his wallet out of his shorts and paid the driver. Rory had a very nice straight nose and a wide, generous, very white-toothed smile. Minus the scruffy hair, too. Ally sighed, watching his dark, neatly cut, very straight hair gleaming in the midday sun. Apart from his height he was also incredibly well built. His massive wide shoulders meant he had to have his suits custom made, huge feet meant his shoes had taken up half the cupboard in the hallway, but somehow in the three years he'd been gone, Ally had forgotten just what an impressive sight he was. She'd even convinced herself that he was fat, that that huge frame would have gone to seed by now, but there he was, literally larger than life and twice as good-looking. A backpack was being unloaded out of the boot now, but so was a suit holder, and despite the shorts and T-shirt there was an air of authority about him she'd never truly noticed before. Rory had clearly done a lot of growing up in the last three years and here he was, about to walk back into her door.

Tanned.

Toned.

And tomorrow he'd be her new boss!

But the fact she'd soon be working alongside him wasn't what was causing Ally's heart to trip into overdrive. Neither was it the fact he was looking even more divine that she remembered. It was all she'd forgotten that terrified her most. Forgotten how just the sight of him flamed her senses, forgotten the agony of loving him from a distance, being a friend when she had wanted so much more.

But no matter how she'd tried, there was one thing time could never erase, one memory that, no matter how hard she'd fought it, simply couldn't be banished from her mind—the fleshy weight of his lips on hers the night they had said goodbye for the last time, the heady, weightless feeling of being held by him, the decadent luxury she had briefly sampled of gazing into those dark green eyes. For one moment in time she had felt like the only woman who mattered but that was followed by the utter devastation the next morning when she had woken up in an empty bed, and realized that the man she'd secretly loved from a distance, the man she'd given her all to just a few hours before, had so easily walked away.

'Rory!' Pulling open the front door, she smiled widely as he dragged his bags up the garden path. 'How are you?'

'Worn out! They kept us for six hours.' Dragging his bag into the hallway, he did a double-take. 'I don't remember the floorboards.'

'They were under that disgusting carpet all along—I found them last year and had them polished up.'

'It looks great. Don't tell me she's still here!' Rory's eyes were practically on stalks as Sheba came waddling down the hall to see what all the noise was, her pink tongue lolling out of her tired mouth, but her old ears pricked up and her tail was definitely wagging as she clearly recognised a very old friend. 'Hey, girl.' Rory dropped down to his knees. 'Hardly a girl, though. How old is she now?'

'Fifteen,' Ally replied, hating the question and all it implied. 'But she's going really well.'

Rory didn't say anything, clearly not convinced by Ally's falsely cheerful voice. Sheba was literally on her last legs, her massive, overweight body barely able to hold her weight, the once gorgeous brown eyes clouded by cataracts now. And deep down Ally knew that, but it was more than she could bear to admit it to herself, let alone anyone else.

'Look, I hate to dash off, but I'm on duty at twelve-thirty…'

'No problem.' Rory smiled, for the first time looking at her, taking in the navy culottes and white shirt, her long dark curls held back in a navy scrunchy, purple epaulettes on her shoulders.

'What do they mean?'

'Associate Charge Nurse.' Ally gave a tight smile. 'Which means I really shouldn't be late.'

'No worries. I'll just grab a coffee and something to eat, and then I think I'll crash.'

'There are coffee beans in the cupboard, but you'll have to grind them.' She gave a tiny wince. 'And I don't think I've got any milk.'

'Doesn't matter.'

'Or sugar.' Ally grimaced. 'And if you want bread, you're going to have to go to the shop, I'm sorry. I didn't know I'd have company.'

'Not a problem.' Rory smiled. 'To tell you the truth, all I want to do is stretch out and sleep.'

'Oh.' Picking up her keys and placing them in her bag, Ally gave what she hoped was a suitably apologetic smile. 'I've just put some washing on. I put some sheets in for you—

they shouldn't take too long, you'll just have to whiz them through the dryer.'

'That's great, Ally, thanks.' A tiny wave of guilt licked at her as she watched his tired face force a smile. She attempted to hide her blush. She looked down at her watch—and Rory got the unvoiced message. 'You'd better get to work, then. We can catch up tonight, and I'll ring out for take-aways....'

'I'm out tonight!' She hadn't even planned to say it, but the lie slipped out so easily it caught even her by surprise. 'But there's some numbers on the fridge if you want to get something to eat...'

'Anywhere nice?'

'Sorry?' Turning at the door, Ally blinked back at him.

'Tonight—are you going anywhere nice?'

'Just out.' Ally shrugged, trying to feign nonchalance, trying so hard just to walk away, but even as she did, a question stilled her.

'It's not a problem, is it?'

'Problem?' Swinging around for the first

time, she managed to actually look at him, her eyes frowning as they met his.

'Me.' Rory looked back at her. 'Being here. If it is, you just have to say. I don't want to…' For a second he faltered. 'I mean, if your boyfriend's going to be worried by my staying here, you just have to say.'

'Why would it be a problem, Rory?' Still she looked at him, even managed a very thin smile. 'I've got an old friend staying for a couple weeks until he finds somewhere else. Why would anyone have a *problem* with that?' She turned and walked to her car. Thankfully the door was unlocked and Ally slid inside. Shaking hands pushed the key in the ignition, and she attempted a smart reverse but failed miserably, instead doing bunny hops the whole length of her driveway.

She'd sit in the movies alone if she had to!

Watch the same film twice over if it kept her out till after midnight.

Anything other than letting him glimpse the effect his return was having on her.

* * *

'Let the poor woman rest!' Rinska moaned, and Ally smothered a smile as the throaty Polish accent sighed into the phone. 'I'll be there when I can.'

'Problem?' Ally checked.

'According to this very eager student, Mrs Williams isn't progressing as she should. He wants me to do another internal to see how far along she is.'

'But she's doing well.' Ally frowned. 'I was only in there a moment ago.'

'How did you find her?' Rinska asked, clearly valuing Ally's opinion.

'Nervous, excited—a typical first-time mum. I told Jake—the student—to suggest a deep bath. She's got ages to go yet.'

'She's only one centimetre dilated.' Rinska rolled her glittery blue-eyeshadowed eyes at Ally. A consultant in Poland, Rinska was now relegated to working as an intern in Australia until her qualifications were approved and, though it must be hellish for Rinska to be such a tiny cog in a big wheel, Ally was delighted to have such a knowledgeable doctor on the shop floor. 'She'll still be labouring when we come back tomorrow morning. She's hoping to do it without analgesia.' A rather loud moan coming from delivery suite two had both women grimacing a touch—well aware that there was a lot of pain still to come! 'Well, at least she's got a chance of making a natural delivery—tomorrow it will be a different story. '

'Tomorrow?' Ally frowned.

'Mrs Williams is already ten days over her due date—from what I've heard, the new registrar that is starting doesn't believe in letting nature take its course. She'd have been put on a Pitocin drip and strapped to a monitor a couple of days ago if he were already here.'

'Are you talking about Rory Donovan?' Ally checked. 'I've worked with him—I guess he tended to err on the side of caution but I always thought that he was really good.'

'He is.' Rinska shrugged. 'At least, according to his stats, all his mothers and babies do well—but his Caesarean rate is way higher than mine.' She gave a tight smile. 'Or rather, what mine was. He's a great doctor, I've no doubt about that, but I doubt he'd have let Lucy go so overdue—that's all I'm saying.

'Do you know him well?' Rinska asked, taking in Ally's rather bewildered frown. Ally gave a sort of vague, noncommittal nod, not particularly sure it would be appropriate to tell Rinska that at this very moment he was probably tucked up in her heavily scented bed! 'We used to share a house.'

Rinska's glittery eyeshadow stretched just a touch further.

'With about three others. I bought a house on the beach when I was a student and over the years I've had more doctors and nurses as housemates than I can count. Rory was one of them.'

'You bought a house on the beach when you were a student—how?' Rinska asked, filling in a patient's notes in her massive flamboyant scrawl as she happily chatted. 'I couldn't afford a beach box, let alone a house.'

'Believe me; it had nothing to do with making an astute investment. A few of us were looking to rent and all the places were absolute bombs. My grandmother had left me some money, not a fortune but enough for a deposit. I saw this house for sale and fell in love with it—it was a bomb as well.' Ally grinned. 'But it was a bomb that was sitting right on the beach, with views to die for! I worked out that if everyone chipped in the rent it would cover the mortgage, and the next thing I knew I was standing at an auction.'

'It would be worth a fortune now.'

'Probably.' Ally shrugged. She had no intention of selling and, anyway, she was far more interested in what Rinska had to say about Rory. 'So what else have you heard about the new reg?'

'Just what I told you. He's more than happy to intervene if nature isn't progressing as quickly as he'd like it to. I wonder how he's going to fit in here?'

'Well, he fitted in fine before.'

'Ah, but he was an intern then.' Rinska gave a dry smile. 'And we all know that an intern isn't allowed to have a single independent thought. I think you should brace yourself for a whole new doctor.'

'Well, we'll soon find out,' Ally answered as casually as she could, scarcely able to believe that in a matter of hours she'd be working alongside Rory again. 'But he surely knows that Bay View isn't exactly high-tech or a high-intervention hospital. If he wants that type of thing he should be working in the city, not at some suburban bayside hospital.'

'Tell him when you see him,' Rinska said as Ally clicked off her pen and closed the patient folder she was writing in. 'What time are you due to finish?'

'In half an hour,' Ally answered. 'I'm just going to check on Mrs Williams's progress and then I might pop in and see Kathy before I give handover.'

'How is Kathy this evening?' Rinska asked,

and Ally could hear the tense edge to Rinska's usually confident voice.

'The same,' Ally sighed.

'Still blaming me?'

'She's blaming everyone now—from the porter who wheeled her to Theatre, to the nurses, the consultant who came in and, yes, to you.' Ally gave a sympathetic smile. 'Rinska, you didn't do anything wrong.'

'I know that.' Rinska gave a tired nod. 'But try telling that to Kathy. Maybe she's right,' Rinska sighed. 'Maybe I didn't make myself clear enough, but I was honestly trying not to scare her too much. I thought she understood how serious the situation was.'

'She didn't want to understand,' Ally said wisely, because even if Rinska was highly qualified, she still needed her colleagues' support.

Kathy Evans was well known to everyone on the maternity ward. She had delivered a healthy baby boy three days earlier but, despite the fact that both mother and baby were doing well, Kathy was bitterly disappointed with how her labour had turned out and was making her feelings known to anyone who cared to listen—and extremely loudly!

Kathy had come in for an attempted VBAC—a vaginal birth after a Caesarean section. When she'd had her first child, the baby had been too large to negotiate the pelvis and an urgent C-section had been performed, much to Kathy's disappointment. A staunch advocate of natural delivery, she had been disappointed that she hadn't been able to achieve one and had been determined that her 'mistake' wouldn't be repeated again. Previously it had been considered that 'once a Caesarean always a Caesarean,' but over the last few years, when appropriate, women had been offered a trial of labour. Things didn't always work out as planned and often women still ended up requiring surgery to deliver their baby, but statistics were encouraging and the tide was starting to turn. Kathy had been determined that she would be successful in her quest to have a natural delivery, had done extensive research in her library and on the internet and was convinced that it was more a question of mind over matter than anything else. But even though her second baby was a much smaller one, Kathy's uterus hadn't contracted efficiently, and after a prolonged labour with minimal progress Rinska had become concerned by some rather ominous signs in Kathy's and the baby's observations and had called in Mr Davies, who had performed an emergency Caesarean section.

'Rinska, you had no choice *but* to call in Mr Davies to perform a Caesarean section. And that's coming from me—one of the strongest supporters in the unit for natural birth and minimal intervention. It would have been considered negligent if you hadn't intervened when you did. You know that!'

'I do know that.' Rinska gave a small tired smile, obviously grateful for her colleague's support. 'I just guess I need to keep hearing it. Over and over in my mind I've gone through Kathy's labour and I really cannot think of anything that I could have done differently, except perhaps explain things a little more clearly to her.'

Ally gave a dubious frown. Rinska, despite her heavy accent, despite the fact English wasn't her first language, always spoke eloquently to the patients, always found the time, even in the most dire of circumstances, to keep her patients informed, and now here she was doubting herself.

Checking that no one was nearby, Rinska spoke in low tones. 'I think she's going to make a formal complaint.'

'Then let her,' Ally said with a confidence that belied how she really felt—even if Rinska was in the right, a formal complaint and the ensuing investigation was a horrible thing for anyone to go through. 'Anyone who looks at her charts will know that you had no choice but to call in Mr Davies, and at the end of the day Mr Davies is the one who operated…'

'I know,' Rinska sighed. 'But it's me she's really against. She was already in Theatre by the time Mr Davies arrived. She says that I panicked and overreacted, that I dramatised the situation just to get him to come in.'

'That's ridiculous.'

'It's also the last thing I need right now. Ally, please, don't say anything, but I'm actually applying for a consultant's position.'

'Here?' Ally beamed and Rinska nodded.

'It's early days, my paperwork isn't quite through yet, but hopefully in a few weeks I can start doing the job I've trained so hard for. It's not that I mind being a resident and having to double-check everything with a registrar who knows less than me…' Rinska gave a low laugh at her own bitter voice. 'Well, a little, perhaps, but it has helped me to learn about the hospital system from the bottom upwards, which can only be good. But it's still been a tough year. And now just when there's an end in sight I'm going to have this complaint to deal with. It's not going to look good for me.'

'You'll be fine,' Ally said firmly, and she meant it. 'When does your shift end?'

'Half an hour ago,' Rinska said wryly. 'I might head over to the social club afterwards. Do you want to come?'

Ally was about to shake her head. The hospital social club wasn't really her scene but the prospect of a drink and a chat with Rinska was rather more inviting than sitting in the movies alone just so that she could avoid Rory, so instead she nodded. 'Sounds good.'

Lucy Williams gripped Ally's hand tightly as Ally rested her hand quietly on the young woman's stomach.

'They really hurt!' Lucy gasped. 'I mean *really,* and the doctor told me that I've got ages to go. Maybe I came in too soon. It's just they were coming so regularly I thought I should be here, and now I find out that I haven't progressed at all!'

'Another one?' Ally checked as she felt Lucy's uterus tighten beneath her fingers. 'OK, don't hold your breath, Lucy. Remember how we taught you to breathe in class…' Her voice was calm and gentle, encouraging Lucy to take some slow deep breaths, talking her through the pain and waiting until the contraction had abated before offering her some much-needed encouragement.

'You *have* progressed,' Ally said firmly. 'I saw you yesterday when you came in for monitoring and you've come a long way since then.' Because Lucy's baby was more than a week overdue, she had been coming into the unit for regular monitoring to ensure that the baby was still active and Ally was telling Lucy the truth—in twenty-four hours she had come a long way. 'The baby is in a great position, and your cervix has thinned out beautifully. Now it's just a matter of letting your body do its job. Remember how I told you that for the baby it's like trying to push its head through a tight jumper?'

Lucy nodded.

'Well, that's what's happening now. I know it can seem disappointing to hear that you're only one centimetre dilated, but this isn't a numbers game. You could dilate quite rapidly from here, or then again the contractions might abate for a while and give you some much-needed rest—but, whatever happens, you're in labour, Lucy, and if you feel you needed to be here, then you're in the right place.'

'So what now?'

'What do you want to do?' Ally asked, not wanting to force her own opinions on her patient. But when Lucy just stared back help-lessly Ally offered a couple of suggestions. 'Why don't you go for a gentle walk around the ward—let gravity help things along a bit?'

'What about when I get a contraction?'

'Lean on Dean.' Ally smiled, looking over at the anxious husband.

'People will think I'm mad! I'm not exactly dignified when I get a contraction.'

'No one will turn a hair—we're all com-pletely used to that sort of thing here. This time tomorrow you'll be watching some other woman doing exactly the same while you're holding your very own baby and thinking, The poor thing. But walking around can help speed things along. After that it might be nice to have a deep bath, which can help relax you and take the edge off the pain.

'Does that sound like a plan?' she asked.

Lucy nodded, and as she heaved herself up out of bed, Ally helped her into a dressing-gown.

'How long are you here for?' Lucy asked.

'I'm off duty soon, but I'll be back at seven in the morning and by then I'm sure that you'll either have your baby or you'll be on the home run!'

'God, I hope I've had it,' Lucy sighed. 'Did I really say I didn't want any drugs?'

'You really did.' Ally grinned. 'But nothing's set in stone in the labour ward!'

Nothing in *life* was set in stone, Ally decided as two minutes after midnight her car pulled up in her driveway, her head still spinning from an evening in Rinska's company. The house was in darkness. Fumbling in her bag for her keys, Ally opened her front door. The first thing to hit her was the smell of cold pizza, the second the deep vibrations of Rory snoring, the third the horrible sting of tears as she slumped on the bottom stair and put her head in her hands.

Rory didn't often snore—but when he did, the house vibrated with each and every agonising breath. So much so that on occasions, when poking and pleading hadn't helped, Ally had sat on this very step playing cards with his latest girlfriend, explaining that this wasn't the norm. Rory only snored when he was seriously exhausted, perhaps after a full weekend on call or on the very rare occasion when he'd had too much too drink. Despite the fact Rory was very much a bloke's bloke, he didn't drink that much, too mindful of his patients to let loose. Rory invariably hit the diet cola, but every now and then he handed over his pager—when his rugby team won the final, which was almost never, and if he wasn't rostered on for New Year and once or twice on his birthday.

She'd sat on these steps with Rory's girl-friends for other reasons too—when Rory had decided to up stumps and move on! Box of tissues in hand, Ally had sat and shivered, listening as a pretty mascara-streaked face had begged Ally to tell her where she'd gone so wrong, attempting to explain that it wasn't them that had the problem—that there wasn't a thing they could change that would make him stay. Rory had told them from the very start that he didn't want to settle down, that he was here for a good time, not a long time.

Her eyes caught on a duty-free bag on the hall table. Frowning, Ally picked it up and read Rory's scruffy unmistakable writing that told her he'd given up and gone to bed, but thought she might like this. Peering into the bag, Ally started at the familiar purple packaging of what had once been her favourite perfume.

Once been, because the day Rory had left, she'd never worn it again.

Pulling open the lid, she aimed a squirt on her wrist, inhaling the heavy fragrance, closing her eyes and dragging it in, the husky, seductive tones evoking memories too dangerous to recall... Rory holding her, the strong, infinitely safe cradle of his arms wrapped around her slender body, the weight of his lips as he slowly explored every flickering pulse point, speaking to her for the first and last times in the intimate tones that were saved for the bedroom, telling her how her perfume drove him crazy, whispering dangerous words as he drove her to a higher place, telling her how the lingering scent of her long after she'd left a room could hold him there a moment longer...

And she couldn't do it, couldn't go there. Rubbing her wrists on her shirt as if she were contaminated, Ally tried to escape the heady smell, tried to slam shut the window of memories he had opened, but the blast was too strong, every recall painful, every memory tainted by his departure—multiplied by his reemergence. Burying her head in her hands, Ally let out a tiny low moan, shook her head and willed it all to stop, but her mind was stuck in some vengeful replay, forcing her to remember the past, forcing her to gaze once again into those green eyes and recall his words.

'You'd be so easy to stay for.'

'Then stay.' Two words uttered in the glowy dew of their first love-making, and even with his bags packed in the hall, the taxi booked to take him away, surely the love they had shared that night and the two words she had uttered should have revealed to him how much he meant to her.

But he hadn't stayed.

Ally could still hear the sound of the shower in the *en suite* that horrible morning as he'd washed away every trace of her fragrance. She could still recall lying in bed and facing the curtains, pretending to be asleep as he awoke, sensing the regret that had drenched his body as he'd replayed the events of the previous night. Quickly, silently he'd dressed and an audible sigh of relief had come from him as the taxi had tooted in the driveway and he'd placed one final kiss on the swell of her shoulder.

Sitting on the stairs, head in hands now, it felt as if for three years she'd been playing some grown-up version of snakes and ladders. Elation at their closeness followed by devastation at his departure—and then the horrible process of regrouping, living in a world where he didn't exist any more. The occasional postcard had been nowhere near enough to sustain her, so she'd focused instead on her work—climbing her career ladder in record time, placing a tentative toe into the murky single world she inhabited, dating even when she hadn't felt like it, clawing her way to the top, where now it was Ally turning down dates, Ally who could pick and choose where she went on a Saturday night. Only for Rory to appear again, only to roll a six and find herself sliding down that appalling slippery slope and arrive back at the beginning.

And suddenly all the game looked was daunting—the thought of starting over incomprehensible.

Two weeks!

He could stay for two weeks and then he'd damn well have to find somewhere else. There was no way she could keep this up, no way he could expect to walk back in and take up their easy-going friendship, to stroll back into her life and take up where he'd left off.

An ironic smile twisted her mouth.

He'd left her naked in bed.

Showering in record time, Ally pulled on a T-shirt and for reasons she couldn't quite fathom she bypassed the G-strings and pulled on the biggest, comfiest, ugliest pair of knickers she could find—knickers her great aunt had sent her one Christmas, knickers that she had meant to throw out, knickers she wouldn't be seen dead cleaning the windows with! Sliding into her cold sheets, she pulled the blankets up to her chin, closing her eyes on this turbulent day, willing sleep to come so that she could function tomorrow. Pulling a pillow over her head, she tried to drown out the noise, then gave in and stared at the ceiling, admitting the truth: it wasn't Rory's exhausted snoring that was keeping her awake—the house could be in silence and she'd still be lying here awake.

It was the overwhelming fact that he was here.

CHAPTER TWO

WAKING up before her alarm, Ally washed and dressed in record-breaking time, layered her lashes with mascara and headed down to the kitchen. Berating the fact she'd flung all the sugar and milk down the sink, and loath to grind beans at this hour, Ally settled instead for a cup of black tea and a slug of honey as she stared at her ancient toaster and willed it to get a move on so that she could hopefully get out before Rory appeared.

The doctors normally started arriving on the ward around eight, an hour after Ally's shift started, but, given it was his first day, no doubt Rory would be keen to make an early appearance. But Ally was determined to be in her car before Rory even hit the shower. Collecting up her pens and stethoscope and slinging her identity tag around her neck, Ally wondered if she shouldn't give him a quick knock before she left. There were no signs of life coming from his bedroom. Normally, or at least a few years ago, Rory would have been up like a lark, noisily hogging the shower, breakfast radio blaring, and Ally wondered if he'd thought to set his alarm clock before he'd gone to sleep.

Of course he had, Ally assured herself. After all, he'd managed to work his way through two pizzas and had written her a note to go with her perfume before he'd gone to bed, It wasn't as if he'd slept round the clock since she'd left him at lunchtime the previous day. And anyway, Ally decided, if he couldn't remember to set his own alarm clock, it was hardly her problem. Closing the front door behind her at a quarter to seven, guilt caught up with her and she re-opened the door, this time slamming it with rather more force than she'd intended, causing her neighbour to frown as he picked up his newspaper from the nature strip and starting every dog in the vicinity yapping as if the postman was about to arrive.

Surely that would shift him!

'I told you that you'd be on the home run!' Walking into the delivery room after handover, Ally took a very agitated Lucy's hand.

'You told me I'd have had it by now!' Lucy shouted, her face red from exertion. 'I can't do this! I want an epidural. Where the hell's the anaesthetist?'

Ally had actually been rostered on for the postnatal ward this morning but, hearing how agitated and upset Lucy had become, it had been decided to do a hasty swap with the nursing allocations—continuity of care was always preferred and in some cases, such as this, essential. Lucy was starting to lose control, her high expectations of her labour— a quick natural birth—hadn't apparently eventuated. Because Ally had seen Lucy on a number of occasions in Antenatal and on her arrival yesterday evening, it had been considered appropriate that she be present for Lucy's delivery in the hope a familiar face might calm her.

'It's too late for an epidural, Lucy.' Ally kept her voice firm, checking her patient's observations and the latest CTG recording and noting that everything was progressing completely normally, though maybe not as quickly as Lucy would have liked. 'You've already started pushing. Your baby's going to be here very soon.'

'It hurts,' Lucy shrieked, fighting the contraction that overwhelmed her.

'Lucy, take a deep breath and push.' Ally's voice overrode her patient's scream. 'Don't waste your energy. Come on, push over the pain…' For a second or two Lucy listened, pushing hard as Ally encouraged her. 'That's it. Come on, push down into your bottom.'

'I can't,' Lucy gasped, lying back on the bed and shaking her head.

'The harder you push, the sooner your baby will be here.'

'It hurts.'

'Because the contractions are working,' Ally said. 'Lucy, nothing we give you now for pain is going to have time to take effect. Your baby is nearly here, and if we give you drugs now it won't help with your pain but it could make the baby drowsy at birth. What about trying the gas?'

'I hate the gas!' Lucy roared, but thankfully as another contraction came, this time she gritted her teeth and bore down as Dean, clearly thankful that things seemed a touch more in control, encouraged his wife to keep on pushing as Ally slowly counted to ten. 'And again,' Ally said. 'You're doing marvelously. Take a big breath and push again!'

She was doing marvellously! In fact, just as Ally was debating whether to give the on-call a ring and let them know they'd be needed in the next hour or so, things started looking rather more imminent. Lucy's shouts were getting louder and her language was getting more colourful as she struggled to get off the bed. The timid woman Ally had got to know was gone now as her baby prepared to make a rapid entrance.

'Get me the bloody anaesthetist!' Lucy roared. 'Or I'm going home this very minute.'

'Good morning!'

So calm and polite was Rory's welcome, so huge his presence as he quietly made his way into the delivery room, that for a minute Lucy literally seemed to forget that she had a baby coming. Her angry face swung towards him, her bulging eyes struggling to focus as he walked over to the delivery bed.

'Lucy Williams, I'm Rory Donovan.'

'The anaesthetist?' Lucy demanded. 'About time!'

'Afraid not.' He gave an apologetic smile. 'I'm an obstetrician. I thought about doing anaesthetics for a while, but I decided that I prefer my patients awake.'

'Well, Lucy's awake,' a terrified Dean said,

nervously shaking Rory's hand. 'No doubt the whole ward is now.'

'From what I hear, she's doing great.' Rory gave Lucy a *very* nice smile and Ally could only blink in wonder as the roaring banshee that had been lying on her back suddenly sat up a touch and even managed a small smile back. 'And if you carry on pushing the way you have been, you'll have your baby in time for breakfast. I saw Win loading up her trolley as I walked past—I can't believe she's still here.' The second part of his comment had been directed at Ally as she opened up a delivery pack but it was put on hold as Lucy bore down again, only this time it was with a rather more concentrated effort, and as she finished he easily resumed the conversation, this time including Lucy and Dean. 'Win's the domestic. She's been here since they put the first coat of paint on and rumour has it that if you deliver before breakfast, she makes the lucky parents toast and eggs any way they want them. Sound good?'

'Sounds great,' Lucy gasped, gesturing for Dean to hand her some ice chips. In the momentary lull Ally headed over to the other side of the delivery room and started to pull up some drugs for the delivery and check the baby warmer.

'Thanks for waking me.' Rory's sarcasm was delivered good-naturedly. 'If your neighbour hadn't had a dog barking the street down, I'd still be asleep.'

'You should have set your alarm.' Ally shrugged, refusing to take any responsibility. After all, she hadn't seen him for three years—it was hardly fair for him to swan back into her life and expect her to suddenly start looking out for him! 'I'm not your mother.'

And as quickly as that the light-hearted banter faded, Ally instantly regretted her words. Rory didn't have a mother; in fact, Rory didn't have any relatives. An only child, his mother had died when he'd been small and his father had lost his battle with cancer just before Rory had left to go to America. Ally had no idea of the circumstances of his mother's death. Rory had only referred to it a couple of times and had always been horribly awkward with her afterwards, insisting that he was well over it, that it had all happened years ago. But, still, her thoughtless comment had clearly hurt and that had never been her intention.

Lord, how she wished somehow that she could take it back!

'I'm sorry.' Her apology was as embarrassed and as wooden as his response. 'I should have known better—I just didn't think…'

'It's no big deal.' Rory shrugged those wide shoulders as if the words had barely registered, but his eyes told her otherwise. 'I'll go and see how Lucy's doing.'

Gently he examined her, sitting down on the bed beside her and talking comfortingly as he performed the rather uncomfortable procedure. Ally watched as the rapport he had so easily created with his patient the moment he had walked into the room grew. Lucy was clearly comfortable with her doctor and that was incredibly important—Ally knew that more than most. In the public health system, rarely did patients get much of a say in what doctor would deliver them. Often, as the doctor arrived for the delivery, there wasn't even time for more than the briefest of introductions. This matter had been addressed at Bay View by the midwifery team, a group of midwives allocated to each patient, looking after the mother during her pregnancy, so that in most cases a familiar face was present at the delivery. But even if Rory's face wasn't familiar, this morning it was very welcome. Dean was listening carefully as Rory explained his wife's progress.

'She's almost there, Dean. Just encourage her to keep pushing. You're both doing a great job.'

'Don't go too far.' Ally smiled as Rory stood up, no doubt realising there was a good half-hour's work before the baby came and ready for a bit of TLC and catching up with Win. 'We might be needing you soon.'

'I'm not going anywhere,' Rory said easily, picking up a newspaper Dean had bought from the mobile trolley, sitting down on the two-seater sofa in the corner and turning directly to his horoscope. 'Do you know what you're having, Lucy?'

'A baby,' she gasped, 'hopefully.'

'A Pisces,' Rory corrected, 'which is the same star sign as me—so you can't go wrong.'

And of all the things she'd remembered, this was one thing Ally had almost forgotten. Forgotten that unlike most doctors Rory didn't just arrive for the grand finale but actually enjoyed the last act. It could have been annoying, a doctor peering over his newspaper every now and then and telling a labouring woman to push over the pain, but somehow it was comforting. That a doctor was here made Lucy feel safe, that he hadn't dashed off and told her the end was in sight. It helped Dean, too, because if Rory thought this display from Lucy was absolutely fine, then maybe, just maybe, it was.

* * *

'Time to get dressed.' Standing up, he pulled on his gown and gloves but didn't intervene, just stood behind Ally's shoulder observing quietly as she attempted to deliver a rather large shoulder. At that moment, Ally was grateful for his calm presence. She felt a tiny beat of panic as she wondered if maybe this baby was too big, if this shoulder was ever going to free. 'Finger behind,' Rory murmured, and it wasn't an instruction, more encouragement when so many doctors would have taken over. 'Got it.'

She could almost feel his smile shining over her shoulder as the baby's shoulders were delivered and the baby uncurled, crying before the rest of its body was even out.

'What is it?' Lucy cried, as Ally placed the tiny bundle onto its mother's stomach. She was grateful that Rory didn't answer, just rubbed the babe's back as mum and dad had the pleasure of finding out. 'A girl,' Lucy gasped. 'We've got a girl.'

'Congratulations.' Rory smiled as the baby's

body pinked with each and every lusty breath, angry fists flailing as Lucy pulled her in closer. 'She's beautiful.'

She really was.

Ally felt her eyes fill as they always did as a new life gave a bewildered blink at the world it had entered. She relished those couple of moments of naked beauty before she wrapped up the babe. Dark strands of hair were plastered to the infant's head, round blue eyes fixed on her mother's, and Ally was in no rush to break the spell. Taking a blanket from the warmer, she wrapped it around mother and daughter as Dean held them both close. She quietly got on with her work, the placenta being delivered easily as the baby suckled.

'I'll come back in a while,' Rory said, slipping away, dimming the lights as he left.

Even that small gesture touched her. Clearly he remembered how she liked to work: the curtains were still drawn and that was exactly how Ally liked it for morning births—the woman had laboured all night, and for a little while the darkness was still welcome. Later either she or Dean would welcome the new day in for the new arrival. Ally tidied up as best she could, recording her two patients' observations as unobtrusively—completely happy with the newborn's progress. Her skin was a healthy pink, her eyes wide as she vigorously suckled. All too soon Ally would have to weigh her, measure her, check her over, then call the paediatrician to do the same. All too soon, the babe would be bathed, the hair that was plastered to her head would become soft and fluffy, the creamy vernix— mother nature's version of cold cream—that covered her now would soon be washed away, but for now she was as new as a newborn got and Ally wasn't about to break this very special moment.

'How are you doing, Lucy?' Ally checked, smiling at the tired, delighted new mother who was too mesmerised by her daughter to even look up.

'She's OK?'

'She's perfect,' Ally said softly, answering every mum's question. 'We'll check her over properly later, but for now she looks wonderful. How are you feeling, Lucy? That's important, too.'

'Tired,' Lucy admitted, then gave an almost apologetic grin. 'I'm starving, actually.'

'Why don't I give Win a call and get the pair of you some breakfast? While you have that, I can weigh and check over this gorgeous girl of yours.'

'Can I hold her for a moment longer?'

'You can hold her for as long as you want.' Ally smiled. 'Win's not as fast as she used to be, so breakfast might take a while!'

Win, as always, timed it perfectly! Just long enough to give Mum and Dad that first long cuddle and just short enough for them not to feel guiltily relieved when Ally took their precious baby off for its myriad of tests while they tucked into tea and toast Win-style—although the eggs Rory had promised were no longer on the menu. Since Rory had last been here, things had changed. Meals were delivered directly from the kitchens, and even though the fridge groaned under the weight of the free-range eggs Win brought in from home, for health and safety reasons they could only be eaten by the staff. As Ally headed into the staffroom for a well-earned cuppa, she found Rory doing just that!

'How are they?' Rory looked up from his mountain of eggs and toast.

'Great. Hugh, the paediatrician, is in looking at the babe now.' Heading for the kettle, Ally's tone was dry. 'I'd hate to know your cholesterol level, Rory. It must be through the roof.'

'Actually, it's very low.' Rory laughed.

'I doubt it,' Ally said, pouring herself a drink and picking up the newspaper—deliberately not turning to the horoscope section, even though she normally did every other day. 'I cleared away *two* pizza boxes last night.'

'Life's bloody unfair like that sometimes.' Rory rained more salt on his eggs as he chatted.

'When I hit the big three-o I decided to take my own advice and get myself checked over properly. I kind of braced myself for a life of salad and steamed fish once I heard the result, but guess what?' Looking up from her paper, Ally rolled her eyes as he continued, 'I'm so healthy I'm almost unhealthy. My blood pressure and pulse rate are both so low it comes as a bit of a surprise that I'm not fainting all over the place, my iron level's great, LFT's completely average, cholesterol low…'

'Lucky you.' Ally poked her tongue out at him then carried on reading her paper.

'What time do you finish?'

'Three,' Ally said, without thinking.

'I'm off at five.'

'Good for you.'

'We could have dinner.'

'I can't.' Ally didn't even look up. 'I've got an antenatal class at six.'

'Congratulations!' Rory grinned. 'You should have told me the news!'

'I'm *teaching* an antenatal class at six,' Ally

said through gritted teeth. 'A mature parents' antenatal class.'

'Which means it will go on for ever,' Rory groaned in sympathy. 'Why is it that the older they get, the more questions they have?'

Ally gave a very reluctant smile at his insight. It was a question she'd pondered many a night when she'd packed up after a class that had run way overtime.

'And they always have a list,' Rory carried on, warming to the subject as he registered her reaction. 'One father-to-be waylaid me in the corridor at work the other week to ask about perineal massage to stop his wife from tearing.'

'So?' Ally frowned.

'He had a list of oils and asked me to choose the one that was most appropriate.' Rory gave her a wide-eyed look. 'I told him to save his money and that a pair of scissors—'

'You didn't!' Shocked, she interrupted, then glared as he laughed.

'No, of course not. I told him that the hundred-dollar oil on the top of his list sounded great, and then I used the sterile scissors a couple of weeks later.'

'Perineal massage works,' Ally retorted. 'You're so anti anything remotely alternative.'

'No, I'm not,' Rory said, mopping up the last of his egg yolk with his toast. 'In fact, perineal massage is way up on my list of re-creational activities…' Green eyes met hers but it was Ally who looked away first, Ally who blushed purple before he continued, 'for parents-to-be. It creates intimacy, gives the mum some much-needed pleasure, but I'm not convinced it reduces the episiotomy rate.'

How had he done that? As Win came into the staffroom, flustered, Ally flicked through the paper and stared unseeingly at an ad for a flash new sports car. Just one pause, one flash of his eyes and a safe medical topic had bordered on dangerous—or at least it had for her. Rory, it would seem, was completely unfazed, his generous grin aimed at Win now as she came to collect his plate.

'I'll wash it, Win,' Rory feebly argued as she

replaced his empty mug with a full one and took his eggy plate. 'It's the least I can do. That was the best breakfast I've had for ages.'

'Don't be daft,' Win chided, but her beaming face said otherwise. 'It's great to see you back here, Dr Rory.'

'Great to see you too, Win.' Rory smiled back, clearly delighted to see her again. 'What's all this nonsense I hear that you're thinking about retiring?'

'It's true.' Win's resigned voice had Ally looking up and she silently prayed that Rory would tread carefully. Win had been the maternity unit's domestic for more than three decades and had run the place with utter devotion over the years. Widowed at a young age and the mother of five children, she had worked a mix of morning and evening shifts to earn enough to raise her children. And in the thirty-five years she had worked on the unit the entire place had remained spotless under her care. Win looked after the patients and staff of the maternity unit way and above the call of duty, cups of tea appearing at busy times, a piece of home-made cake coming out during quieter ones. But way more valuable than the tea and cake was Win's insight: on more occasions than Ally could recall, she had found Win chatting to an anxious mum, somehow putting a woman at ease in the way only the voice of wisdom could. Many times the powers that be had tried to get Win to sign a new contract, to schedule her hours in line with the rest of the health network, but she had stood firm, keeping to the old rules. But now Win couldn't do it any more. She couldn't manage the forty-hour weeks, and reducing her hours would mean signing the dreaded contract, which could see her allocated to any ward in the hospital.

'I need to cut down my hours. I was hoping to just do one shift a week—you know, to keep my hand in—but if I do, my supervisor has told me that they won't be able to guarantee that I'll be rostered here on the maternity ward. She's spoken with management and they said I'll have to go to wherever I'm needed most if I'm only working one shift a week. I could end up on A and E perhaps or maybe even Intensive Care, and that's the last thing I want.'

'A change is as good as a rest,' Rory offered, and Ally just wished he'd drop it, sucking in her breath as he pushed on. 'But if you don't want to go to another ward, just tell them that you belong here,' Rory said, as if it was that easy. 'The ward will back you. After all, you've been here longer than I've been alive. Surely the hospital should bend over backwards to accommodate you, shouldn't they?' He looked over at Ally, clearly expecting her support. 'Have you spoken to Win's supervisor about this?'

'Of course I have,' Ally answered, but her eyes were warning Rory to drop it. Ally, along with most of the senior staff on the maternity ward, had been vocal in her efforts to keep Win, but the sad fact of the matter was that she was considered too old and too inflexible for the job.

The truth, though Win didn't know it, was that the powers that be knew full well that Win couldn't bear to work anywhere other than her beloved maternity ward, and that was the very reason they weren't offering it—they wanted her to leave! It had been left to Vivien, the maternity unit manager, to soften the blow a bit, to explain to Win that despite the staff's protests, if she signed the new contract, there was no guarantee she'd be working on maternity.

Once Win had gone, Ally half expected Rory to pick up the conversation where it had been before Win had come in—to tease her a little bit more—but Rory had other things on his mind.

'Did you really speak to her supervisor?' Rory checked.

'I just said so, didn't I?' Ally answered abruptly.

'So why can't she stay?' Rory pressed.

Ally wished he would just leave it. 'Rory, I

did speak with her supervisor, so did Vivien, so did Mr Davies, the consultant, but, as much as we all adore Win, that's not the issue.'

'Win's been here—'

'Win's been here for more than thirty years,' Ally broke in. 'Which is exactly the problem. Win runs the ward as she did when she started. She refuses to change her routine.'

'Why should she,' Rory answered, 'when clearly her way works?'

'It doesn't any more, though,' Ally snapped. 'Take the eggs! The days are gone when you bring food in from home and give it to the patients. As nice as it is to spoil the mums, there are health regulations that have to be followed, and for ages Win refused to abide by them. Over and over the staff tried talking to her, telling her that she couldn't keep cooking for the patients, but she refused to listen. It took two written warnings—'

'Written warnings!' Rory's voice was incredulous. 'Over eggs on toast! You know when I applied for the registrar's position here, I was sent a load of stats, and one of the things that stood out was the infection control rate. This may be a relatively small suburban hospital but the infection rates in this ward are second to none. That has nothing to do with luck, you know, Ally.'

'I know that,' Ally flared, surprising even herself at her defensive stance. 'But you're not aware of all the circumstances, Rory.'

'Enlighten me, then,' Rory answered, but Ally shook her head. She stood up and for the first time in living memory she didn't pick up her cup and put it in the sink, she just left in on the table, 'Why should I, Rory? You can't just disappear for three years and then swan back and expect nothing to have changed.'

'Of course things change,' Rory answered, but Ally wasn't listening.

'You disappear for three years and then expect to swan back and pick up exactly where you left off. Well, like it or not, life goes on with or without you. Rules change, people change…' Stupid tears were pricking at the back of her eyes and Ally swallowed hard to keep them in. 'And I'm sorry if you come back and don't like what you find, but if you were that concerned about Win and her blessed eggs then you shouldn't have left in the first place!'

There was this horrible, prolonged silence. Knowing full well that she'd gone too far but refusing to back down, she glared at him with angry eyes and her lips set in a pale rigid line until finally Rory responded.

'This isn't about Win, is it?' There was a distinctly nervous edge to his voice as realisation dawned. Looking across the room at his shocked expression, Ally did the only thing she could in the circumstances: gave a tiny half-laugh and shook her head.

'I guess not.'

'Is it about...?' He didn't finish his sentence, but he didn't need to. The appalling discomfort that filled the room was stifling now.

'Just forget it, Rory,' Ally attempted, but she knew it was futile. How could she ask him to forget something she so clearly couldn't? 'It's just…' Raking a hand through her hair, she stumbled to find the right words. 'I can't pretend it didn't happen.'

'No one's asking you to,' Rory pointed out. 'Ally, I wanted to talk last night.'

'Last night?' An ironic grin twisted on her mouth. 'Three years after the event! Well, that's fine, then, why didn't you just say so? Rory, just because you've had more girlfriends than I can even recall, just because you can walk away so easily, it doesn't mean that I can. We shared a house for years and if you learnt anything about me in that time, surely it was that casual sex wasn't exactly my forte!'

'Ally don't…' Rory shook his head. 'There was nothing casual about that night.'

'Oh, I beg to differ.' Tears weren't threatening now, tears weren't even close. Her eyes glittered angrily as she stared back at him. 'You didn't even wake me up to say goodbye. You were in that taxi and on the way to the airport before the sun had even come up. And even allowing for my comparatively high standards, I'm sure you'd agree that one tatty postcard four months later merits the word *casual!'*

'Ally.' Crossing the room, he faced her. 'We both knew at the time it wasn't going to work…' It was Rory stumbling over his words now, Rory attempting to do the one thing he wasn't very good at—let a girl down gently, 'We both wanted different things.'

'Meaning?' Ally frowned. Maybe she didn't want the answer to the question she was asking, but after three years she knew that she needed it, needed to somehow find closure.

'Look at you,' he said, doing exactly that, the space between them disappearing as he placed his hands on her shoulders and stared down at her. The first physical contact in three long years and her body seemed to unfurl beneath him. His touch, which had been so absent, was now so wonderfully familiar and it hurt, literally hurt, not to respond, to just stand there and feign nonchalance as each pore, each cell awoke from dormant hibernation. Somehow she stared coolly back at him as Rory delivered an extremely well-rehearsed speech.

'We both wanted different things,' Rory said softly.

Ally attempted to open her mouth and mimic the words as he delivered them, because it was the same speech she had heard recited by his tearful ex-lovers as she'd comforted them, and now it was being aimed at her. But Ally was brutally aware that, unlike those times, there was no one outside waiting with a box of tissues, no one to sit on the stairs with and hold her hand as she digested her loss. Not only were they sharing a house but she had to work with him! She would have to face Rory, work alongside him for months, years even, so she took it with all the dignity she could muster, and held tears firmly in check as Rory attempted to let her down gently.

'Look at you, Ally,' Rory said again. 'You're an idealist…'

'What?' *That* wasn't part of his usual recital. Maybe he'd picked it up in America. Perhaps he'd added a few more lines to his pep-talk!

'You have this amazing vision, Ally. You're devoted to your career, your home. You know exactly where you're going—'

'What on earth has that got to do with anything?' Ally questioned, watching as Rory's forehead creased in exasperation.

'I guess what I'm trying to say is what happened that night—'

'Will never happen again!' Ally broke in, and finished this difficult, uncomfortable conversation. 'I wouldn't necessarily describe myself as an idealist, Rory, but I do have standards—and what happened that night didn't reach them!'

'You're upset—'

'No,' Ally interrupted. 'I'm not upset—I *was* upset at the time. Not just with you, Rory, but with myself. It was stupid to jeopardise a good friendship because we were both feeling a bit emotional. It was stupid to go to bed with a guy who's a self-confessed commitment-phobe. You're right, we do want different things. A quick roll in the hay because it feels right at the time just isn't for me. Frankly, I expect better from myself.'

'But not from me?'

Ally didn't even bother to answer that one. 'I just want to make one thing very clear: I hope we can work well alongside each other, be friends again even, but what happened that night was a mistake—and one I have no intention of repeating.'

'Fine,' Rory answered, and even if his body didn't move a fraction she felt the welcoming breeze of distance between them. She could finally manage to breathe again as the guidelines were firmly established. 'Would it be easier if I moved out? I can ring the doctors' mess now…'

'There's no need for that.' Ally shook her head, managed a smile even as she went on, 'So long as I've made myself clear.'

'Clear as crystal.' Rory gave a tight smile.

CHAPTER THREE

GLANCING down at her watch and seeing that it was well past eight, Ally let out a tired sigh as the last of her antenatal class departed. As she and Rory had jokingly predicted, the session had gone way over. Fiona Anderson a forty-year-old primi gravida, or first pregnancy, who was expecting her baby in just a few days had commandeered every question-and-answer session. She had been accompanied by her equally anxious husband, Mark. Every explanation Ally had given, they had pushed for more information; every positive comment she had made they had questioned, throwing up worst-case scenarios and demanding to know what would happen and generally terrifying the rest of the class! Ally was tired, hungry and, despite being the bubbly, effusive midwife as she had held the class, all she really felt was drained. As much as she loved her antenatal classes, loved the chance to get to know the women on a more personal level, to build a relationship long before they hit the delivery room, sometimes Ally wondered if her job was just a touch too consuming. The emotional energy she put into each and every patient sometimes left her feeling depleted, and tonight that was exactly how she felt.

Depleted.

She wearily pressed the rewind button on the much-viewed video of childbirth she had played to her class tonight and tried to summon up the energy to pack away and go home. She'd dodged Rory last night and after their little tête-à-tête in the staffroom, she was sorely tempted to ring Rinska and hit the social club again rather than face him tonight. But she couldn't. Rory would know she was avoiding him, might even guess that she was still incredibly uncomfortable around him, and more than any of that, Ally simply didn't have the energy to stay out again tonight.

Hearing the door open, Ally turned around as Fiona's nervous face peered around it.

'Sorry, Ally, I know you must be in a rush to get off. I wanted to mention it in class but Mark said that I'd just scare the other parents if I said…' Fiona stared down at her rather large stomach, her hand nervously caressing the baby inside. 'I'm just so worried.'

As tired as she was, looking at Fiona's anxious face, Ally pushed all thoughts of fatigue and facing Rory firmly away. From the questions Fiona had been asking in class, there was clearly something on her mind and if Fiona didn't feel secure then Ally's job wasn't yet done. A positive frame of mind was essential for labour and with their baby so close to its due date, Fiona was right to come back and talk to her midwife, to voice whatever was on her mind. 'Where's Mark?'

'In the car. I told him to wait there for me there while I spoke to you.'

Ally's smile was genuine as she smiled warmly at the nervous woman and waved for her to come back in, her only goal being to put her patient's mind at rest.

'Do you want to call Mark in? I can talk to you both.'

'No, thanks.' Fiona sniffed.

'So what's worrying you?' Ally asked, steering her to a seat and flicking the kettle back on.

'One of the women from our antenatal class had her baby a couple of days ago. We went to visit her before class, to say congratulations and have a peek at the baby. We've become friends, I guess.'

'Kathy?' Ally checked, immediately realising the problem.

'She says she's going to sue the hospital, that she's going to ring up a current affairs show and write to the newspapers.'

'I'm sorry you had to hear all that.' Ally

gave a sympathetic smile, but her heart sank, thinking of poor Rinska if Kathy followed through with her threats.

'I didn't say anything in class because I thought I might scare the other mums-to-be, but Kathy is appalled at what happened to her, and so am I. Kathy wanted to have a natural delivery, she was adamant that she was going to have her baby without drugs.' Fiona wrung her hands in her lap, and Ally could see that she was close to tears. 'Yet she ended up having a Caesarean section when she didn't even want one. Kathy said that the doctors and nurses just took over, that they refused to listen to her wishes. The doctor didn't even speak English very well and Kathy couldn't understand what she was telling her. She was practically forced to sign the consent form for the operation...' Ally didn't interrupt, mindful of patient confidentiality. There wasn't an awful lot she could say, and it was also important that Fiona get everything off her chest, voiced all of her concerns, before Ally jumped in. 'Mark and I are very committed to a natural delivery,' Fiona gulped. 'I haven't taken so much as a headache tablet throughout my pregnancy, I didn't even take the iron tablets the doctor suggested, I chose to get my vitamins from natural sources, and my iron levels have been fine throughout...' Defiant eyes jerked to Ally's, her voice turning from anxious to assertive, but Ally had been in midwifery too long not to notice the fear behind her words. 'I don't want my labour to turn out like Kathy's. I don't want some doctor who doesn't even know me telling me what to do with my body.'

'Fiona, I understand how upset you are, I really do,' Ally emphasized, as Fiona gave her a disbelieving look. 'I understand how disappointed Kathy is, too,' she continued, treading very carefully. 'You know that I can't discuss specific cases with you, and I'm certainly not going to go through Kathy's labour with you just to defend the hospital or put your mind at rest, but what I can tell you is that I'm also a strong advocate of natural birth—as any of my colleagues will tell you. I'd be disappointed if I didn't have a natural delivery, but at the end of the day the goal is a healthy mother and baby—that has to be our first priority.'

'I understand that,' Fiona nodded, 'but I just don't want anyone rushing in…'

'No one's going to rush in,' Ally assured her. 'But you have to listen to me when I tell you that no two deliveries are the same—and if that sounds like a platitude then I make no apology. No one can guarantee that you're going to have a natural, drug-free birth, but what I can guarantee is that the staff will do everything they can to give you the chance to have one if that's what you want.'

'It is.' Fiona took a deep breath. 'We tried for five years to get pregnant, Ally. This baby is something we both dearly want, and we want to do this right.'

'And you will,' Ally said firmly. 'This is your baby, your delivery and everyone at Bay

View is going to do their level best to ensure a happy outcome for both mother and baby. We'll keep you up to date with what's happening and the doctors and midwives will give you the information you need to make informed and sensible decisions—'

'Like they did with Kathy?' Fiona asked with more than a hint of sarcasm.

Ally shook her head. 'Fiona, as I said before, I'm not prepared to discuss Kathy's labour with you. You're just going to have to try to trust that—'

'Trust!' Fiona snapped the word back at her. 'You're talking like I've got a choice here?' And Ally knew not to take it personally— knew that Fiona was terrified of losing control of her body, that seeing Kathy so bitter and depressed would have been upsetting.

'I'm sorry.' Fiona ran a tired hand over her face. 'I'm sorry for taking this all out on you when you've been nothing but kind to Mark and me. It's just I'm so scared of anything going wrong. I've been waiting to have this baby for ever and now that it's nearly here, I'm...'

'Terrified?' Ally offered, slipping an arm around the tense woman as Fiona gave in to her fears and had a little weep. 'Nervous, too?' Ally said, elaborating a touch when Fiona nodded. 'And incredibly excited, too, I'll bet.' Handing Fiona a wad of tissues, Ally let her weep for a moment longer. 'You're going to be OK, Fiona,' Ally said assuredly, resting one hand on Fiona's large bump. 'You both are.'

'Promise.'

But Ally couldn't really promise that. Both she and Fiona knew that deep down, but hope and faith were powerful drugs and they were the two drugs Ally had no qualms about handing out to pregnant women when they were called for.

'You're going to be fine,' Ally said assuredly. 'And in just a few short days you'll be holding your baby.'

* * *

'You're late!' Rory frowned as Ally wearily put her bag down on the hall floor. 'Not that it's any of my business, of course,' he said quickly, and Ally gave him a tired smile.

'I *am* late. What's that smell?'

'Veal escargot,' Rory said. 'Or it was an hour ago. It's probably burnt.'

'You made dinner?' Ally frowned, slipping off her shoes and padding into the kitchen, her tired eyes taking in the appalling mess—the onionskins and mushroom cartons on her bench, a trail of cream dripping its way from the container to the stove top. They told her that this wasn't a prepackaged meal and she blinked in surprise at her house guest. 'You actually *made* dinner?'

'I did.' Rory grinned. 'I even singed the hairs on my arms trying to light your stove,' He held up a rather large forearm for her inspection. 'I'm surprised that I've got any eyelashes left.'

'Don't go borrowing my excuse.' Ally smiled and it was so nice not to have to explain about her constant battle with her eyelashes, so nice that he knew her well enough at least to know that.

'So what's the occasion?' Ally asked as Rory pulled a bottle of wine out of the fridge.

'Old friends,' Rory answered, filling two glasses and handing her one. 'And how very important they are. I'm sorry that I didn't keep in touch while I was away, Ally.'

'I know.' Avoiding his gaze, she chinked his glass with hers. 'It's good to have you back. You didn't have to do this. I didn't even know that you *could* do this!'

'You haven't tasted it yet,' Rory pointed out.

'It doesn't matter what it tastes like,' Ally sighed, happy to sit down and be spoiled, because even Rory's burnt offerings would surely beat the buttered crumpets she'd envisaged toasting. 'I'm starving.'

'How was the antenatal class?' Rory asked as he drained the potatoes with one hand and took a sip of his wine with the other. Even with a teatowel over his shoulder, he somehow managed to look divine.

'Long,' Ally answered, turning her attention to her own wineglass, determined not to be caught staring. 'I'm all for antenatal education and women getting to know each other and sharing each other's journeys, but sometimes I think that there should be an exclusion zone placed around the women who have just delivered, like the signs they have in X-Ray, warning heavily pregnant women to stay away.'

'What happened?' Rory asked, joining her at the table and placing her plate in front of her.

'I've just had a mum grill me about every worst-case scenario for labour. She went through everything from shoulder dystocia to external version and, no matter how hard I tried to steer her, she insisted on details, wanting to know what the staff would do for *this,* wanting to know the hospital policy on *that.* And I know exactly why she's so terrified. Did you meet Kathy today? Failed VBAC—'

'It looks nice, Rory,' Rory interrupted, attempting a very poor impersonation of a female voice. 'Oh, look, you even put a sprig of fresh parsley on top!'

'Why,' Ally asked with a very resigned sigh, 'do men have to be praised when they cook as if they'd performed some amazing feat? I said thank you!'

'No,' Rory shook his head. 'You didn't.'

'I'm sure that I did,' Ally said through gritted teeth, cutting up her veal and popping a piece in her mouth and then blinking. 'It's lovely! Really lovely, in fact...'

'You don't have to go overboard,' Rory grumbled. 'A simple thank you would have done.'

'Thank you,' Ally said. Looking at him for the first time since that morning, she managed a genuine smile, appreciating coming home to a meal and conversation. As nice as it was, the food and wine didn't matter, even the fact that Rory didn't feel the same way that she did was almost bearable. It was just nice having him here, having him back, even if it was for just a little while.

'So what's Kathy been doing?' Rory asked, picking up the conversation where he'd dropped it. 'No, let me guess. She's been scaring everyone with horror stories of her appalling labour, how she was practically forced into signing the consent form...'

'Pretty much,' Ally sighed. 'I know Kathy's disappointed. Hell, I'd be the same...'

'Would you?'

'I'd be disappointed.' Ally nodded. 'Devastated, actually, if I had to have a Caesarean, but I hope I wouldn't take it out on everyone. I mean, she's not only upsetting the staff with her wild accusations, she's upsetting the other patients.'

'She needs to be told.'

'We can't censor her!' Ally gave a half-smile. 'I wish we could. Fiona—the patient I was talking about earlier—told me that Kathy's writing to the papers and trying to get on a current affairs show.'

'So she can spread her depression a little bit wider?' Rory gave an angry shake of his head. 'What annoys me the most is the way everyone at work is pussyfooting around her.'

'I suppose no one wants their name added to the complaints list.'

'Well, she can add mine. I'll talk to her tomorrow.'

'You can't,' Ally said, appalled. 'Rory, I wasn't joking when I said that we can't censor her! You can't tell her not to voice her opinions, for goodness' sake!'

'No,' Rory said. 'But I can make her opinions a touch more informed. She's lucky that her baby's OK. I was looking at her notes and charts and, as far as I'm concerned, the only thing Rinska did wrong was not calling in Mr Davies earlier.'

'Don't tell Kathy that!' Ally yelped.

'I wouldn't,' Rory said, irritated. 'But Rinska gave her every chance for a so-called "normal" delivery. If I'd been the doctor on duty, she'd have been in Theatre a lot sooner.'

Rory gave an annoyed shake of his head then grimaced. 'We're going to stop this conversation right here—we are not to talk shop!'

'Sorry,' Ally groaned, but Rory waved her apology away.

'I'm the one who asked about work, but at the end of the day we haven't seen each other for three years!'

'True,' Ally admitted, taking a nervous slug of her wine, because even though Rory was right, even though there should be a million and one things to talk about other than a difficult patient on the wards, work was her safety net, or at least it was tonight. 'So what brings you back to Melbourne?'

'It's home,' Rory answered with simple honesty. 'It took me a while to work it out, though. When my dad died, I convinced myself that there was no reason to stay, that I didn't have any family here so what was the point? I'm probably not making much sense…'

'You are.' Ally took a sip of her wine. 'I'm

not pretending that I know how you felt, though. I come from such a massive family I can't imagine being the only one left...' Biting her lip, Ally cringed a touch at her own directness, but Rory just smiled.

'I'm not going to burst into tears and do the poor little orphan routine, Ally. Dad died three years ago now. And I don't know if a thirty-year-old really qualifies as an orphan!'

'Stop it,' Ally said, hating the way he made light of things. She'd meant what she'd said. She literally couldn't imagine what it must be like to be Rory. When his father had been dying, night after exhausting night Rory would come home after visiting his father, tell Ally how he was doing as he grabbed something to eat and then go to bed. For Ally it had been the saddest part of the whole wretched time: no list of aunties or cousins or brothers or sisters to ring; no gaggle of relatives to bring up to date. Just Rory dealing with it all alone.

'You're too sensitive, Ally.' Rory laughed,

watching as her eyes brimmed with tears. 'But the funny thing is, it took a couple of years of being away from it all for this place to really feel like home. It's not just family and a house that make you feel as if you belong some-where—it's all the memories, all the people you grew up with, all the people you've actually forgotten you know. I'd go to the mall in the States and I missed the strangest things: not banging into someone I used to play footy with; or seeing someone that I used to go to school with and wondering what the hell they've been up to. You know the kind of thing I mean—having a chuckle to yourself at how bald or fat or miserable they look now, or laughing with them for five minutes about the things you used to get up to.'

And Ally thought about it for a moment. Like it or not, she could barely make it to the end of the street without bumping into someone she knew. There were several rows of relatives filling the local phone book and, as much as it annoyed her sometimes, as much as she craved privacy sometimes, she wouldn't change her world for anything.

'How's your love life?' Ever direct, Rory changed the subject swiftly as he went straight to the point. 'I heard through the grapevine you were engaged last year.'

'No!' Blushing, embarrassed, Ally attacked her veal with her knife and fork.

'To Jerard Hawkins.'

'No,' Ally said again, absolutely refusing to go there. 'We were never engaged.'

'Thank heavens for that. I really couldn't see you two together.'

'Why not?' Intrigued, annoyed at his assumption, Ally forgot that she didn't want to talk about it. Her voice was brittle when she spoke. 'I suppose you don't think I'd make a very good cosmetic surgeon's wife.'

'Come to think of it—no.' Rory smiled as her jaw dropped. 'You're so against anything remotely invasive, I really can't imagine you surviving one of Jerard's cosy little dinner parties where they're talking about the latest advances in breast augmentation or the Brazilian butt lift.'

'It's an entirely different field to maternity,' Ally responded tartly, though privately she agreed with every word Rory was saying. Even though Jerard was highly skilled and did some amazing work, the bulk of his income came from invasive and, in Ally's opinion, often unnecessary procedures. As hard as Ally had tried to be interested, after a long, hard and sometimes emotionally draining day in the delivery ward, sometimes it had been hard to even muster a sympathetic groan when Jerard had grumbled about his workload that day—hard to pretend to listen to his cosmetic triumphs when a baby had just died.

Rolling her eyes, Ally admitted the truth. 'You're right, I wouldn't have made a good cosmetic surgeon's wife.'

'I never said anything of the sort. I think you'd make a dazzling trophy wife for Jerard…' As Ally opened her mouth to argue, Rory overrode her. 'I was referring to the fact that, although admittedly I haven't seen him in years, I always found Jerard to be the most boring person I've ever had the mind-numbing experience of meeting. At least I think he was—I tended to fall asleep in mid-conversation.'

'Jerard isn't boring!' Ally retorted.

'He must have had a personality transplant, then. He's arrogant, too. Do you remember that time we had a party here…?' Rory carried on, warming to his subject. And even though it had been Ally who had broken things off, even though she hadn't gone out with Jerard for months, she still felt duty bound to defend him.

'Jerard isn't boring or arrogant,' Ally said. 'At least, I never found him to be, although I admit, when he doesn't like someone, he does have a rather uncanny knack of dismissing them…' Wincing at her own words, Ally froze in mid-sentence.

'So Jerard doesn't like me.' Rory winked as Ally's cheeks flamed.

'I didn't say that.'

'You did,' Rory delightedly pointed out. 'You said just that.'

'You always do this,' Ally bristled. 'You always manage to drag things out of me, make me say things that I never intended to.'

'I know!' Rory gave a triumphant smile. 'So come on, Ally, what did I do to offend Jerard?'

'Apart from sleeping with his girlfriend?'

'I slept with you three years ago, for heaven's sake, long before Jerard was on the scene.'

'I wasn't talking about me.' Ally squirmed in her seat as the dreaded taboo subject somehow reared yet again. 'Heaven forbid that Jerard should have a problem dating one of your exes, that would practically rule out the female population of Melbourne!'

'Then who?' Rory asked in an intrigued voice, and Ally swore she could hear his brain ticking as he mentally worked his way through his little black book. 'Come on, Ally, who am I supposed to have slept with?'

'I'm not discussing this, Rory,' Ally flustered, wishing she hadn't had a glass of wine when she was so tired, wondering how on earth Rory always managed to prise information out of her. But as determined as she was to end this conversation, as much as an in-depth discussion of Rory's formidable sexual conquests was the last thing Ally wanted or needed, anger overrode sensibility. 'I can't believe you could cause so much upset without so much as a shred of guilt. I can't believe you don't even remember!'

'Uh, we are in Australia, and I believe that means I'm innocent until proven guilty.' His eyes frowned in mock concentration. 'What were the charges again?'

'Amber Rodgers,' Ally flared, appalled that he genuinely didn't seem to know. 'The ICU nurse. And her—'

'Amber!' Rory's jaw dropped open, but only for a second. A mischievous smile played on his lips as Ally screwed her eyes closed, her face the colour of the wine she was holding in her hand. 'And her friend!

Oh, Ally.' He started to laugh. 'Is that what Jerard told you?'

'It wasn't just Jerard who told me, the whole hospital knew about it. You left poor Jerard at a party and went with both of them back to Amber's. How was he supposed to take her back after that little public display in humiliation?'

'"Poor Jerard"!' Rory stopped laughing but a smile was still twitching on his mouth. 'On the night in question, your honour…' Ally's lips pursed in indignation as Rory continued in his mock police officer's voice. 'I attended a function in the doctors' mess. Due to the fact I was on call I chose to partake only in orange juice. At around ten p.m. I'd had enough and decided to leave. It was at that point I witnessed Jerard and two young ladies arguing in the foyer… It's like Cluedo, isn't it?' Rory added, reverting to his normal voice.

'Stop it Rory,' Ally interrupted, but annoyingly Rory carried on.

'The young lady was very tearful, your

honour, and she asked if I could take her and her friend home—to which I agreed.'

'I'll bet,' Ally snarled.

'During the car journey home, it became apparent that Jerard had, in fact, discovered his girlfriend and her friend in a rather compromising position…' He paused, sat in delicious silence his face split into a massive grin as Ally's eyes widened. Her eyes jerked to his, her hand going over her mouth as Rory gave a slow affirmative nod. 'Do you see now why Jerard was more than happy to lay the blame on me?'

'You're telling the truth?' Ally checked.

'I'm telling you what happened,' Rory corrected. 'I dropped the girls at Amber's house and, no, I didn't get asked in for as much as a coffee.'

'Oh, my goodness.' Ally blinked.

'Tell me something, Ally,' Rory said picking up the forgotten dinner plates and heading over to the sink as Ally sat and digested the rather interesting news. 'How many girlfriends do you think I've had?'

'Sorry?'

'Well, your recollection of my wild youth seems a lot more colourful than mine.'

'Oh, come on, Rory, you can't kid me.' Ally let out a rather undignified snort. 'I shared a house with you!'

'For how long?' Rory asked.

'Three years.'

'Three years.' Rory nodded, scraping all the leftovers onto one plate. As he went to throw it into the bin, just as Ally opened her mouth to halt him, Rory remembered of his own accord, calling Sheba over and loading her bowl with the remains of dinner. As the old dog limped over, her tail wagging, Ally watched, touched that he'd thought to spoil her. 'And in those three years how many women did I date?' He didn't wait for her response. Instead, he answered his own question. 'Two.'

'Two!' Ally let out another undignified snort, followed by an incredulous laugh, but Rory's back was to her now, blasting on the taps and filling the sink before continuing.

'Maria, gorgeous as she was, came with two impossible parents who considered three months of dating quite long enough and demanded that I do the honorable thing by their daughter.'

'She adored you,' Ally reminded him. 'She was devastated when you broke it off.'

'So was I.' Rory shrugged, washing the dishes as he chatted. 'But I was twenty-four, for heaven's sake. I had no intention of settling down and I certainly wasn't ready to make bambinos, which was what her parents wanted!'

'What about Gloria?' Ally prompted. 'You were together for two years. Why did you break it off with her?

'I liked someone else,' Rory replied, with an honesty Ally couldn't really argue with. 'It didn't seem fair to drag things on when I knew it wasn't going to go anywhere.' Throwing the teatowel on the surface, he joined her back at the kitchen table. 'And that's my checkered past. As good as it was, it wasn't *that* good.'

'What about that blonde woman I found in the kitchen one morning, buttering *my* crumpets and wearing *your* T-shirt?' Ally said, bristling at the memory—they'd been her last two crumpets after all. 'Mandy, that was her name.'

'She'd just broken up with my mate, Paul, for crying out loud,' Rory replied. 'If you'd bothered to set your alarm that morning, you'd have found her asleep on the sofa ten minutes before. I'm not that low, Ally.'

'Well what about…?' Ally's voice trailed off, frowning at her own recollections. Surely there had been more. How many parties had they had? How many times had she found women in floods of tears in the kitchen, or locked in the loo having hysterics, or chain smoking on the patio, because Rory had turned them down?

Turned them down.

And Rory, it would seem, had somehow, despite the appalling odds, managed to swing the jury with his skilled delivery, beyond *rea-*

sonable doubt starting to creep into Ally's confused mind.

'Two!' Rory said again, just to ram home the fact. 'I hate to shatter your illusions.' Rory gave a low laugh. 'Hate to shatter mine, actually. Look, Ally, there's a lot of gossip that flies around, a lot of innuendo, you know that as much as I do. Most of the time I just laugh it off. If that's what people want to think of me then let them—they don't know me after all. But you do,' Rory added, and Ally could have sworn she heard a tiny hurt note in his voice. 'Surely you know I'm not like that? That I'm not into that type of thing?'

'What type of thing?' Ally asked, wondering if he'd have the gall to actually say it. The mist cleared from her mind. She absolutely refused to be drawn in, angry with herself that for a second there she'd almost believed him, that Rory had almost had her convinced.

'One-night stands.' Rory's eyes held hers. Unlike Ally, he didn't appear remotely embarrassed by the conversation.

'You've got a nerve Rory…' She wasn't even angry, just tired of his games, tired of the roller-coaster ride of emotion Rory constantly took her on. All she knew was that she wanted to get off, had had enough of Rory Donovan and his mind games for one day. Shaking her head, Ally stood up. 'Thank you for dinner, Rory. I'll let Sheba out for a couple of minutes then I'm going to bed. Remember to set your alarm in the morning. I'm on a late shift so I doubt I'll be up.'

'Don't worry.' Rory yawned. 'I'll be up this time.'

Even though she was still annoyed with him, Ally felt a proper apology for her earlier thoughtless words was still in order. 'I am sorry for what I said earlier, about not being your mother—it was beyond thoughtless.'

'Ally, it was a totally normally thing to say—you're not the first and you certainly won't be the last.'

'Perhaps,' Ally sighed. 'But given that I know…'

'Forget it.' Rory smiled. 'And don't worry about Sheba. I'll see to her—I might even take her for a stroll on the beach.'

'She can't walk far.'

'A stroll,' Rory said, 'not a power walk.'

'She'd like that.' Ally gave a pale smile. 'Night, then.'

''Night, Ally.'

Padding down the hallway, she ached for the safety of her room, ached to throw herself onto the bed and let out the breath that was bursting in her lungs. Her emotions were swinging like a pendulum. The fact he was here, back in the house they had shared, chatting and joking with her, it was almost as if the years he had been gone had melted away somehow. And yet she was furious, too— furious that he could just look her in the eye and lie, deny the absolute truth. They'd even discussed it that morning, for goodness' sake, but as she walked away he called her.

'That one doesn't count!' Rory said, clearly reading her mind, but Ally didn't turn around, just stood still in the darkened hallway with her back to him, tears stinging her eyes because it had counted, had counted so much more than he would ever know.

'I guess not,' Ally managed, heading again for her door, turning the handle as Rory continued.

'That night doesn't count as a one-night stand, Ally…because it meant something…'

CHAPTER FOUR

IT WAS a relief to hear the door slam in the morning, to no longer have to lie in silence. Acutely aware of Rory in the next room, Ally had woken up at the first beep of his mobile alarm, had lain gritting her teeth as over and over Rory had hit the snooze button, before he'd finally dragged himself out of bed and into the shower.

And noise shouldn't worry her. After all she had shared her house with more people than she could instantly recall, but no matter how she tried it was hard to relegate Rory to house-mate status. Smiling into the darkness, she'd listened as he'd attempted quiet, listened as he'd spoken in low, gentle tones to Sheba then ruined it by stubbing his toe in the darkness and bouncing off the walls. She'd listened as he'd boiled the kettle and snap, crackled and popped his way through breakfast. And even if it was the same, it was different—his pager bleeping as the sun rose, the sound of his low voice as he gave his orders into the phone.

Snapping on Sheba's lead, Ally led her very reluctant dog along the beach path.

'Come on, Sheba,' Ally urged, trying to muster some enthusiasm. 'You love a paddle.'

Just not today.

Sitting down on the sandy shore, Ally watched as an exhausted Sheba attempted a lethargic sniff at the water's edge.

Ally loved this time of the morning—too late for serious joggers and dog walkers and way too early for sunbathers and mothers with toddlers. Just an elderly couple walking arm in arm, picking up shells and stabbing a stick at the odd washed-up jellyfish, a couple of surfers heading for home. But apart from that, it was empty.

This time last year, Sheba would have loved it. OK, Ally admitted. The dog wouldn't have been riding the waves but she'd have been splashing her tired old body in the salty water and proudly dragging back a piece of drift-wood for Ally to inspect. Now she could barely make it to the beach. Sometimes Ally was sure she merely attempted a frolic to appease her, but this morning she didn't even try that, just sniffed at the water then waddled back to her Ally, resting her old grey head in Ally's lap, thumping her tail silently on the sand as Ally idly stroked her head, listening intently as her mistress laid the blame squarely at Rory's feet.

'Did he keep you out too long last night, Sheba?' Ally stared down at her loyal friend. 'Believe me, I know all about it!

'Well, don't worry, he's not going to be staying with us for very much longer...' Ally's voice trailed off. She stared out at the glittering water, taking nourishment from the view that always calmed her, and she needed calming. Her stomach had been curled into a ball of tension since Rory had reappeared, her mind reeling from the impact of seeing him again, from the jumble of conflicting emotions he so easily evoked. God, why wasn't this sorted? Ally begged herself. Why three years later was she sitting on the beach with Sheba at her side, pondering the conundrum that was Rory Donovan? Why had he had to come back now? Why couldn't he have come back and found her totally anaesthetised to his charm, her diary bulging with engagements?

A tiny whimper from Sheba reminded Ally that she wasn't an entirely hopeless case. If it hadn't been for the fact that Sheba was on her last legs, she wouldn't have even been home when Rory had called. The reason she wasn't sunning herself on the beach in Queensland with her friends Becky and Donna this week was because there was no way she could have put Sheba in a kennel. Even though her mum had offered to come in and feed her, Ally knew that Sheba would have spent the entire fortnight fretting.

'Come on, Sheba.' Standing up, Ally waited for Sheba to join her, watching as she heaved her body up then with a shudder lay back down. 'Sheba, please.' Sinking to her knees, Ally tried to cajole Sheba into standing. 'Come on, honey, you can't lie here all day. It's just a few steps back to the house. Come on, Sheba.'

As she stood so too did Sheba, panting as she walked back to the house. Once inside Ally poured her some cool water but she was too tired even for that. Stretched out on the wooden floorboards, Sheba's chest rose and fell rapidly and no matter how hard over the past few weeks Ally had tried not to think about it, she knew now that she had to. She knew that Sheba had been for her very last walk, that she was too old, too tired and in too much pain even to walk the few steps down to the beach now.

But she was eating, Ally thought hopefully. Only last night she'd gobbled up the remains of dinner, and Rory *had* taken her for a walk last night. It wasn't any wonder she was worn out today. Pouring a glass of water for herself,

Ally drank it with a trembling hand, a touch more reassured, especially as Sheba's breathing started to slow down to a more regular rate. But as she headed off to the laundry, as much as she tried to ignore it, her eyes seemed to be drawn to the vet's business card stuck on her fridge. She wondered how she could ever bear to use it, but knew in her heart of hearts that Sheba couldn't go on like this for much longer.

'What are you doing in here?' Rory frowned, peering into the storeroom where Ally was hiding halfway up a ladder and dusting off shelves. Rostered on for the ward that afternoon, Ally had been hoping for a busy shift to take her mind off things, but the one time she needed action the place was quiet. There were no new admissions expected from the delivery suite, no women in early labour to be monitored and all babies were out of the nursery and being proudly shown off to visitors. Most of the staff were making the most of the rare quiet time and sitting around the nurses' station gossiping, Rory included. But Ally hadn't been remotely in the mood for light-hearted chatter and had taken herself of to the massive storeroom to tackle a job she had been putting off for ages.

'I'm trying to make some room in here,' Ally answered, barely looking down. 'The new extension starts in a month and Vivien wants all the old admission record books to be filed in here.'

'Why?'

'I don't know,' Ally answered, 'and I don't really care. She asked me to make a start on it when I had a moment and that's what I'm doing.'

'Is everything OK, Ally?' Rory asked, and the concern in his voice wasn't helping at all. Her nose started to run, a precursor to the tears that had been threatening since that morning. 'You seem a bit flat.'

'I'm fine.' Concentrating on keeping her voice steady, Ally gave the shelf she was cleaning another needless spray of detergent.

'You're not avoiding me, are you?'

'Avoiding you? Rory, why on earth would I be avoiding you?' Tears dried up, annoyance taking over now.

'I don't know,' Rory admitted. 'Maybe I said something last night…'

'Rory, I know we're friends and everything and, yes, it's great to see you again but, believe it or not, I do have a life that doesn't revolve around you.'

'I know you do. I just thought you seemed a bit upset.'

'I am!' Her brown eyes flashed as she spoke. 'And guess what, Rory? It has absolutely nothing to do with you!'

As the door closed behind him Ally carried on with her furious cleaning, refusing to even *think* about him. How dared he swan in and assume that just because she was upset, just because she was a bit flat, it was about *him?*

On the plus side the shelf space was organised in record time. Her rage had made her productive, but on the down side there was no reason at all to stay in the storeroom and she damn well wasn't going to give Rory the satisfaction of thinking she was avoiding him. At least the afternoon observations were due, and Ally made her way around her patients, checking the mothers' and babies' observations. Only Kathy Evans didn't have any visitors, and as Ally walked into her room, Kathy quickly took Toby off her breast and did up her nighty.

'Don't stop on my account.' Ally smiled, picking up the baby's chart and pulling out her pen. 'How long did he feed for?'

'I didn't time it,' Kathy answered tartly, pulling a blanket around her babe. 'Unlike the staff here, I don't have one eye on the clock. Toby feeds when he's hungry. I'd sleep when he did if there wasn't someone constantly coming in to check up on me.'

'Has he had dirty nappies since I was last in?' Ally asked, deliberately ignoring Kathy's argumentative tones.

'Just a wet one,' Kathy said, grimacing slightly as she tried to turn herself to get out of bed.

Knowing she would probably be shot down in flames for even offering, still, Ally put down the chart and offered her assistance.

'Would you like me to put him down for you, Kathy?' In a surprising move from the very bristly, independent lady, Kathy rather reluctantly relented, handing over her infant and watching closely as Ally checked his observations and filled in his chart, then took a moment to settle him in his cot, soothing the restless babe to sleep.

'How are *you* feeling this afternoon?' Ally asked, as Toby started to settle.

'I'll be fine when I get home. The doctor this morning said I need to be in for a couple more days but I want to get Toby home.'

'Five days is around average for a Caesarean section,' Ally said. 'I just need to check your observations and take a look at your wound and your breasts.'

'I'm OK,' Kathy bristled. 'I've just fed my son and I'd like to get some sleep, please.'

'I ought to do your obs, Kathy,' Ally pushed. 'And then if you like I can pull the curtains and leave you to doze. I can put a sign up on your door so that the domestic doesn't disturb you when she brings round afternoon tea. I can ask Win to save it for you if you'd prefer.'

Slightly mollified, Kathy nodded. 'OK,' she sighed. 'Do my obs, but can we save the breast and wound checks for later? I've just got comfortable.'

'Sure,' Ally reluctantly agreed, fiddling with the buttons and pressing the start button on the machine. 'How's the breastfeeding going?'

'It would be going a lot better if I didn't have a massive scar on my stomach and a drip in my arm,' Kathy snapped. 'I hate to think of the drugs I'm passing on to Toby.'

Frowning as she saw Kathy's rather elevated blood-pressure reading, Ally pulled her stethoscope from around her neck and checked it manually this time, but the reading was the same, if anything a bit higher.

'Is there a problem?' Kathy asked.

'Your blood pressure's a bit on the high side, Kathy. Do you have any pain—'

'Could you just tell me the reading, please?' Kathy broke in. 'I don't need to spoken to like a five-year-old!'

'It's one hundred and seventy over ninety,' Ally answered calmly, refusing to rise to Kathy's provocative tone and popping the tympanic thermometer into her patient's ear. 'And your temperature is elevated too—it's thirty-eight degrees,' she added without waiting for Kathy to ask. 'I really ought to have a look at your stomach.'

'So that the doctor can do the same again in ten minutes' time?' Kathy snapped, and Ally gave up trying to reason with the woman.

'I'll go and let the doctor know.'

'Well, can you make sure that it's not Rinska?' Kathy said tartly as Ally headed for the door, her shoulders stiffening as Kathy's hostile tones continued. 'If my blood pressure's up and that woman comes near me, I'll probably end up having a stroke!'

'Problem?' Rory asked as Ally came over to the desk.

'Kathy Evans is hypertensive—one hundred and seventy over ninety; she's febrile, too, at thirty-eight degrees.'

'How's the baby?' Rory asked, turning rapidly to the baby's obs chart, nodding in relief at the stable readings. 'His obs all seen fine.'

'He's OK,' Ally agreed. 'He's demand-feeding and has had plenty of wet nappies.'

'Have you checked her blood pressure manually?' Rory asked, reading through the observation chart.

'Yep.' But as Rory scanned the drug chart his expression changed.

'Why hasn't she had any painkillers? She hasn't even had paracetamol! Did you ask if she was in any pain?'

'Of course I asked,' Ally retorted. 'But

Kathy didn't appreciate being spoken to like a five-year-old and neither do I! I do know basic nursing care, Rory, but the simple fact is that her obs are unstable and she refuses to answer any of my questions, let alone allow me to examine her wound site or breasts.'

'I'll go and see her,' Rinska groaned, putting down her biscuit and coffee and clearly bracing herself for another confrontation with this most difficult patient. Ally shuffled uncomfortably for a second before speaking, unsure how to say what she had to in front of so many staff.

'It might be better if Rory saw her, Rinska.'

'Has she refused to have me look after her?' Rinska's voice was strained, her cheeks flaming with embarrassment as Ally gave a slightly helpless shrug.

'She did ask to be seen by someone else,' Ally said as tactfully as she could. 'And, given the circumstances, it's probably for the best.'

'I agree with Ally,' Rory responded. 'Ms Evans clearly needs a thorough examination, not, of course, that you wouldn't give one but she's hardly compliant at the moment.' He gave an exasperated sigh. 'Has anyone told this woman how lucky she is to have a healthy baby?'

'She doesn't want to hear it at the moment,' Ally said. 'Rory, going in there with all guns blazing isn't going to help matters.'

'I have no intention of going in with *all guns blazing,*' Rory retorted sharply. 'But clearly pussyfooting around the issue isn't helping. The staff are all terrified to go in there in case their name's added to Ms Evans's long list of complaints…'

'I've been in to see her regularly,' Ally flared, but Rory gave an impatient shake of his head.

'I'm not talking about you, so don't take everything so personally. I don't even want to go in there and watch her scribbling down every word I say, but the fact is we have a patient who's clearly unhappy and not feeling at all well, combined with nurses and doctors who did everything right feeling as guilty as hell for no good reason. I think this needs to be sorted out once and for all.'

'Leave it, Rory.' Rinska shook her head. 'I don't need you to fight my battles—you'll only put her off side and end up with a complaint against you as well.'

'They can't sue you for being honest.' Rory gave a tight grimace. 'Yet! Ally, go and tell Ms Evans that I'll be in shortly, I just want to have another look at her notes before I see her.' Oh, how she wanted to warn him, to tell him to leave well alone, but Rory wasn't the intern he had been three years ago. He was a registrar now and the choice was entirely his. But maybe he saw the anxiety in her eyes, because he looked up and gave a tight smile. 'Don't worry, it will be fine.'

And with that she had to be content. Taking a deep breath, Ally knocked on Kathy's door and went in.

'Dr Donovan will be along to see you shortly.' Ally managed a smile and, mindful of Rory's words, realising that perhaps, given Kathy's hostile attitude, some basics might have been missed, Ally tried a fresh approach. 'If you buzz me next time you feed Toby,' Ally offered, 'I can come in and show you a couple of positions that might make things a bit more comfortable for you, given that you've had a Caesarean. Sometimes resting the babe on a pillow—'

'You don't have children, do you?' Kathy interrupted, glaring at Ally, who shook her head. 'Well, I've been feeding Lily for three years now. I'm still feeding her at bedtime so I certainly don't need to be shown how to feed my own child by someone who's never even held her own baby—'

'How are things?' Rory waltzed into the room, ignoring the palpable tension, and introduced himself to Kathy. 'I'm Dr Rory Donovan. I'm the obstetric registrar on this afternoon. Sister Jameson told me that you had a temperature and that your blood pressure's elevated. Do you have any pain?'

'Ally already asked me that,' Kathy answered tightly.

'I know,' Rory responded. 'And you didn't answer her question either. I see you haven't been taking any of the analgesia that's been ordered for you. Are you concerned that any medication that you take will be passed on to your baby?'

'Someone has to be.'

Rory didn't rise to the bait, but Ally saw one of his eyebrows rise an inch. 'I'd like to examine you, Kathy. I need to have a look at your stomach wound and listen to your chest, but first I'd like to ask you a few questions.' He ran through several diagnostic questions and each was answered with a grudging negative until Rory washed his hands and asked her to lie down.

Ally positioned the blanket as discreetly as she could and watched as Kathy clamped her lips together and extremely reluctantly lay back. Rory gently probed her abdomen. 'Your wound looks fine. Do you have any tenderness here?' Gently he pushed and Kathy shook her head. 'Or here?' Another shake of her head. 'OK, let's sit you up and I'll listen to your chest.' He held out his hand to assist her up but Kathy didn't take it, choosing instead to use the monkey pole above her bed to raise herself. Ally watched as the woman tried to hide her obvious pain.

'Some nice deep breaths, Kathy.' Rory put on his stethoscope and listened to the back of her chest. 'Can you just undo your nightdress for me, Kathy, so I can listen to the front?'

'I'm fine,' Kathy bristled, but when Rory stood firm she undid the front buttons of her maternity nightdress and not by a flicker did Rory's expression give away what he was thinking. But Ally wasn't faring so well. A frown puckered her brow as she caught sight of Kathy's cracked, bleeding nipples. One breast was red and swollen and Ally was furious with herself that she hadn't been more insistent with Kathy. Regular breast checks were routine on the maternity ward, but each time Kathy had been approached she had withered the staff with some cutting comment, basically refusing an examination each time. At the end of the day that was her prerogative and Ally couldn't force her patient to be examined, but seeing how much needless pain Kathy was in was upsetting. Rory concentrated on his patient's breathing, first moving his stethoscope across her chest before wrapping it around his neck and washing his hands again. When he came back to the bedside, Kathy closed her eyes as supremely gently he examined her painful, engorged breasts.

'How long have they been sore, Kathy?' Rory asked.

'For a couple of days,' Kathy finally answered. 'Well, the nipples have been sore for a couple of days, but the pain in my breast only started this morning.'

'Can you lift your arms a little, please?'

More compliant now, Kathy did as she was asked, and Ally was pleased with Rory's very low-key, matter-of-fact response to Kathy's problem. Mastitis and sore, cracked nipples were extremely commonplace in the post-partum period, but Kathy's case was rather extreme and the fact she had let it go on without telling the staff was worrying.

'You have mastitis in your breast, Kathy and the start of an abscess.' Rory pulled her night-dress closed as he explained the problem to Kathy. 'Some of your glands are swollen in your axilla, you must be in a lot of pain.'

'It's not too bad.'

'What about your nipples—have you tried a shield when you're feeding?'

'I can't use them.' Kathy's voice was brittle again, her eyes staring fixedly ahead, refusing to look at either Rory or Ally.

'I'm going to need to take some blood from you.'

'Is that necessary?'

'Very,' Rory said. 'I want to take blood cultures so we can hopefully isolate the bacterium and give you the appropriate medication. We need to get you started on some broad-spectrum antibiotics—'

'No.'

'Kathy, you have an infection—'

'I'm not taking antibiotics,' Kathy furiously broke in. 'I know that they pass through the milk, they'll give Toby thrush. I've asked my husband to bring me in some cabbage leaves to put on my breasts—that should help.'

'It will help.' It was Ally talking now. 'We've got some in the fridge on the ward. A lot of the mothers use them to ease the discomfort of engorged breasts, but as Rory has said you've also got mastitis and an abscess—you need antibiotics—'

'I *need* to be left alone. If your colleague hadn't rushed in and performed a Caesarean, I'd have been home now, instead of picking up bugs in hospital. Now you want me to take yet another drug, to clear up yet another problem you lot have created. And when my baby gets thrush, no doubt you'll prescribe yet another drug to clear that up as well. You lot stand here dictating *my* treatment for *my* body and I'm just supposed to lie here and say thank you. Well, unlike the way I was treated in labour, I demand input, I demand to make informed choices—'

'Kathy.' Rory's voice was quiet but firm, halting the woman's angry tirade. 'Let's clear the air, shall we?'

'Meaning?'

'Meaning that since you had your baby, you've been extremely vocal in criticising the hospital and a number of my colleagues.'

'I'm making a formal complaint,' Kathy snapped.

'Which is entirely your prerogative. If you feel that you have been mistreated or that the care given to you was negligent, it is right that you complain. Now you've refused to discuss your issues with Mr Davies or Rinska or any one of the midwives.'

'I don't want to hear their excuses.'

'Fair enough. Well, the problem we face now is that you need treatment. In fact, you've needed treatment since yesterday, yet you don't trust the staff enough to tell them when you're unwell. As you've said, I believe on numerous occasions, you want to be fully informed—so that's what I'm going to do. Ally, could you hand me Kathy's medical notes, please?'

Oh, she didn't want to. Ally didn't like the way this conversation was heading one single bit, but Rory held out his hand and completely ignored Ally's slightly anguished, warning look.

'I understand that you were keen to have a vaginal birth.' Rory was reading as he spoke. 'And it says in your antenatal notes that on several occasions you were warned that it might not be possible.'

Kathy stared up at the ceiling, her face set as Rory pushed on.

'You went into spontaneous labour at two p.m. and came into hospital around nine p.m. This was your baby's heart tracing on arrival to the ward.' He handed the slip of paper over to Kathy who, after a very long moment of stony silence, reluctantly took it. 'The heart rate looks fast, but babies' hearts beat much faster than adults, this is a completely normal tracing. The line beneath—'

'Is my contractions. I'm not stupid.'

'I know you're not,' Rory answered, and continued to explain Kathy's labour to her in detail, as she continued with her stone wall of silence.

'This is your baby's heart rate when Rinska decided to perform an emergency Caesarean.' He handed her the tracing but Kathy didn't take it. 'There are decelerations, a lot of them—that means that the baby's heart rate was slowing down during contractions, and as the trace goes on, if you looked then you'd see that they become more and more prolonged. Toby was taking longer and longer to recover from each contraction.' Ally noticed that he had personalised things now, was referring to Toby, not 'the baby', and she watched Kathy's jaw clenching as Rory pushed on. 'Toby was in foetal distress. He wasn't receiving the oxygen he required. In fact, by the time you reached Theatre, Toby's heart rate was barely picking up at all between contractions.' He pulled out another CTG recording and this time Kathy took it, listening in silence as Rory pointed out the variances on the tracing.

'She didn't tell me this…'

'She told you that the baby was becoming distressed.'

'Yes.'

'That it was imperative to deliver the baby?'

'Yes.' Kathy nodded. 'But she didn't explain all of this to me. I had no idea how serious it was.'

'So you didn't understand that if Toby wasn't delivered immediately, he might suffer permanent brain damage or possibly die?'

'She didn't say that.'

'Did you want her to?' Rory asked.

'Yes. No.' Kathy gave a tiny sob. 'I don't know.'

'This trace was taken at five-thirty a.m.,' Rory said, 'and this one was taken at five to six. Your baby was born at six a.m., Kathy. Toby had to be born, there was no choice but to perform a Caesarean. Now, if the doctor didn't give what you consider an adequate explanation, it would have been for one of two reasons. Firstly, she didn't want to terrify a laboring woman with the worst possible scenario when she knew that if the baby was quickly delivered it could be avoided. And, secondly, given that she had to call her consultant, and arranging theatre time would have been a factor, Rinska didn't have time to sit at your bedside and go through all the tracings. Rinska also knew that you were extremely well versed in the risks and would have been told the reasons that might precipitate a Caesarean section. In my opinion the fact that English isn't her first language didn't enter the equation—the doctor was simply busy saving your son's life.'

'If she'd just let me go for a little bit longer,' Kathy insisted, but Rory remained immovable and shook his head.

'The cord was wrapped tightly around Toby's neck…'

'She could have cut it,' Kathy said.

'It was too tight for him to move down,' Rory said, and gave her a moment for that information to sink in before continuing. 'Maybe I'm just a guy, maybe I'm horribly insensitive to a woman's needs, because, while I'm aware that many women want to have a natural birth, I don't really understand it.'

Kathy frowned, as did Ally, and Rory gave a hint of sheepish smile. 'Like I said, I'm a guy and a doctor and I can't really get my head around the pain part of it, but I'm happy to be educated, more than willing to listen to my patients and as far as possible give them the birth they want—'

'Give them! That's exactly my point,' Kathy interrupted. 'You're a privileged spectator in a natural process—'

'And one who's not remotely politically correct,' Rory broke in, and Ally was amazed to see the first hint of smile break on Kathy's strained mouth. 'What I don't get is the "at all costs" part.' The smile on Kathy's face faded, and she gave a strangled sob. Tears poured down her face as Rory gently continued, 'Hell, Kathy, you've got two beautiful, healthy children, you've done so amazingly well, you should be so proud.'

'I feel such a failure,' Kathy admitted. 'I wanted so badly to do it naturally.'

'You couldn't!' Rory's words were brutally honest. 'But it doesn't make you any less their mother, any less a woman. Just be glad you live in these times, Kathy.'

But Kathy shook her head, refusing to be comforted, refusing to believe it was that simple.

'I'm saying all this, Kathy, not because I want to stop you from making a complaint— as I said before, that's entirely your prerogative. I'm doing this because you need to understand what happened during your delivery, you need to get your head around those facts so that you can start to trust us again. Because if you don't, you'll refuse treatment, you'll endure a massive, preventable infection that might make you seriously ill and, in my honest opinion, if you carry on with this guilt and blame, you're going to end up with severe postnatal depression.' As she opened her mouth to argue, Rory steamed on ahead. 'A difficult labour, post-delivery complications, a mother with high expectations…you have some of the classic warning signs. If you won't take antibiotics for an obvious infection, am I right in assuming that down the track you'll be refusing anti-depressants?'

'I don't need them,' Kathy said through gritted teeth.

'No,' Rory agreed, 'you don't—yet. Right now you need to understand what happened and start enjoying your beautiful baby—and he is beautiful, Kathy. Very beautiful.'

Kathy was crying in earnest now. Used to tears on the maternity ward, Ally recognised them for what they were—not bitter or angry, but sheer exhausting, emotive sobs that had been held in for way too long. She moved to comfort Kathy, but Rory got there first, placing one strong hand on her heaving shoulder and letting her weep for a while before speaking.

'Will you take the antibiotics, Kathy?'

'Can I still feed Toby?' she gulped.

'You can.' Rory nodded. 'But, like you said, there's a good chance it could cause oral thrush. I see in your notes that you've got some expressed breast milk in the fridge. I could take the blood now and hold off starting the antibiotics till this evening, give you a chance to express some more milk. If you're happy to do so, perhaps Toby could survive on the bottle for a few days. We've got teats that simulate a nipple, so he shouldn't get too used to it. However, that's more Ally's department.'

'He's so young, he should go back to the breast fairly easily,' Ally agreed. 'And you can stay in here till you're happy that your feeding's established.'

'But I'm supposed to be going home in a couple of days.'

'Not with an infection,' Ally said. 'And not until you're confident that Toby's feeding well—which I'm sure he will be.'

'I've actually got some more breast milk in the freezer at home.' Kathy looked over at Rory. 'If I ring my husband and tell him to bring it in…'

'You've got some stored at home?' Rory asked, and Ally held her breath, hoping that Rory wouldn't blow things now. 'How come?'

'Kathy is still breastfeeding her daughter, Lily. I guess she wanted to be prepared.'

Rory could have given a wide-eyed look that she was feeding her three-year-old, could have said any number of things to upset Kathy in this rather labile mood, but, instead of making things worse, his face spilt into a wide grin of admiration and he made things suddenly a whole lot better.

'What a woman!' He grinned. They were exactly the words Kathy needed to hear today. 'I'll go and pull up those antibiotics, then!'

CHAPTER FIVE

'I'll go.' Glancing up at the call bell display and seeing it was Kathy buzzing, Ally handed over the sleepy infant she had just finished feeding at the desk to the student Jake.

'Thanks.' Jake gave a grateful smile, clearly relieved not to have to see why Kathy was ringing. Since Rory's little *talk,* Kathy's door had remained firmly closed, and although Ally had been in a few times to check her drip and observations, exhausted after her tears, Kathy had slept for most of the afternoon and into the evening.

'Hi, Kathy.' Ally came into the room but, mindful that Kathy would have just woken up, she didn't flick on the overhead light, just turned on the nightlight switch. 'How are you feeling?'

'Better,' Kathy admitted. 'Those painkillers really helped a lot. Toby is starting to stir—can I get his milk from the fridge?'

'I'll prepare that for you if you like,' Ally offered, half expecting a refusal but pleased when Kathy nodded. 'Sometimes babies can be a bit tricky taking a bottle from Mum,' Ally warned, hoping not to alarm Kathy but wanting her to be prepared. 'They can smell the milk from their mums and have trouble getting the hang of the teat. Toby might be fine, given that it's your milk he'll be having, but if you want, and only if you want, we're more than happy to feed him for you.' Sure Kathy would immediately shake her head, Ally was pleasantly surprised when Kathy continued to listen. 'We could give him a couple of bottles tonight if you like and let you rest properly and tomorrow, once the antibiotics have kicked in and you've had a good sleep, you'll be—'

'That sounds great.' Kathy didn't even let Ally finish—a new woman indeed after

Rory's little pep-talk! 'Actually, I'm so anti bottlefeeding him, it would be a relief tonight if someone else could do it for me.'

'We'd be happy to.' Ally smiled, gazing down at Toby who was starting to make his presence felt, sucking furiously on his fat little fist. Kathy was a lot happier now but still quite tearful, and Ally didn't push, letting Kathy take the next step but delighted with the progress that had been made.

'He looks hungry,' Kathy observed. 'If one of the nurses could feed him, would it be OK if I had a shower?'

'The water will help a lot,' Ally agreed, wrapping the blood-pressure cuff around Kathy's arm as she chatted. 'And then I'll bring you in some cabbage leaves. Your blood pressure's normal now,' Ally said, turning the machine towards Kathy so that she could see the reading for herself. She popped the tympanic thermometer into her patient's ear and got an instant reading. 'So is your temperature—it's amazing what a good sleep can do.'

'And the right drugs.' Kathy gave a tight smile.

'Would you like some dinner? I've saved your supper tray in the fridge.'

'I'm not really hungry.' Kathy shook her head.

'Some sandwiches, then?' Ally offered.

'Maybe later…' Kathy gave a small shrug and, sensing that her patient was feeling awkward, Ally decided to broach what they were both avoiding.

'How are *you* feeling,' Ally said, perching herself on the bed, 'after speaking with the doctor? Do you have any questions?'

'Not really,' Kathy answered. 'He made things pretty clear.' Looking up at Ally, she qualified it with a small smile. 'I like direct, don't worry.'

'I'm not worried,' Ally said, 'just concerned—for you. I know I don't have children of my own, but I do understand your desire for a natural birth.'

'It wasn't going to happen for me. I guess I just didn't want to admit it—I wanted to blame everyone else instead of myself.'

'Why does anyone need to be blamed?' Ally asked gently. 'I was speaking to Rory—Dr Donovan—just before he went off duty and he said that part of the reason you were feeling so awful was that you've been through the equivalent of two labours.' Ally paused for a moment to let her words sink in. 'A long and painful labour and then a big operation. He was telling me that's one of the reasons he's not particularly keen on VBACs—around half the women end up working twice as hard!'

'I've never thought of it like that.' Kathy blinked.

'You've experienced labour, Kathy,' Ally said gently. 'Several gritty hours of it. And then you had to go through surgery. You're allowed to feel washed-out!'

'It doesn't give me the right to be an utter bitch, though. I've been awful, haven't I?'

'You've been a challenge.' Ally grinned. She stood up as Toby started to cry in earnest. 'Shall I take him down to the nursery?'

'Ally?' Rinska's nervous face popped

around the door. 'I'm sorry to disturb you, but you have a phone call.'

'Thanks, Rinska, I'm just coming.'

'Rinska.' Kathy's voice was strained and high and even in the subdued lighting Ally could see she was blushing. 'Could I have a word with you, please? I want to apologise.'

Wheeling her precious cargo down towards the nursery Ally didn't rush to take her call, assuming that it would be the nursing co-ordinator to check on the bed status or a relative with a patient enquiry. Instructing the staff to feed Toby and then to take him back to Kathy for a cuddle, Ally headed to the nurses' station and picked up the telephone. 'Sister Jameson speaking.'

'Ally!' Instantly recognizing Rory's voice Ally frowned into the phone, wondering why he had specifically asked to speak to her. If it was to do with a patient, there were more senior nurses on, or surely he could have checked with Rinska. 'What time do you finish?'

Ally's frown deepened further as she glanced at her watch. 'In an hour or so. Why?'

'Are you coming straight home?' His voice was light, his words casual, but it only confused Ally further and she didn't immediately answer. 'I was just wondering if you were going out after you shift, or if things had got busy.'

'Why?' Ally asked again, choosing Rory's direct approach, tired of the games that he seemed to be playing with her. 'What does it have to do with you?'

'Nothing.' Rory didn't sound so casual any more, his voice unusually hesitant as he carried on talking. 'It's just…'

'Just what, Rory?' Ally snapped. 'I was actually with a patient when I was called out to take a telephone call—only to find out that it's you asking whether or not I'm coming straight home. What's going on?'

'It's Sheba!'

The high horse Ally had just leapt onto bucked her off with the two words Rory delivered and galloped off into the distance, leaving Ally reeling, trying to grab the reins.

'What's wrong with Sheba?'

'Ally.' Rory's voice was calm. 'She's OK, well, when I say she's OK she's in her basket having a sleep, but when I got home she was crying—she'd had an accident. I've cleaned it up and I carried her outside, but she's not right. I think you ought to come home when your shift's finished, that's all. I didn't want to worry you—I just thought you ought to be here.'

'The vet came and saw her this morning.' Ally's voice was thick as she struggled to get the words out. 'He gave me some painkillers. Could you give her one and I'll get off as quickly as I can?'

'I've already given her one,' Rory said. 'Come home, Ally.'

And it wasn't just Sheba that had her weeping as Ally replaced the receiver, but the fact Rory had carried her, had thought to give her a tablet, and that twice in their short conversation he'd referred to her house as home.

'What's wrong?' Jess was over in a second.

'Nothing,' Ally attempted, then gave in. 'It's Sheba. Apparently she's not very well. I know she's only a dog…'

'Go home,' Jess said without hesitation, because even if it was just a dog, it was Ally crying, Ally who never called in sick, Ally who was always the first to get to work and the last to leave. 'The night staff are already arriving—go home.'

Negotiating the short drive home, Ally flew up the driveway her heart in the mouth as Rory opened the door.

'She's the same,' he said immediately, wrapping an arm around her and leading her up the path. 'I'm sorry if I scared you, Ally. I didn't realise that you'd already called the vet out. Maybe she's no worse than when you left her.'

But Sheba was. Rory's arm stayed around Ally as she walked down the hall and into the kitchen, gripping her tighter as Sheba managed a few thumps of her tail as Ally made her way over.

'She's never had an accident. She'd be so upset.'

'I've cleaned it all up,' Rory said as Ally knelt down beside her best friend and stroked her tired head. 'Like I said, I carried her outside and she had a wee. She should be OK for tonight and I'll take her out again in the morning.'

'Poor thing,' Ally gulped, watching Sheba's rapid breathing. 'What should I do?'

'What did the vet say?' Rory asked, practical as ever.

'He was going to come on Sunday,' Ally choked. 'He's known Sheba all her life. He said we should have Saturday…' Ally shook her head. 'But she's worse, I don't think it would be fair to leave it till then.'

'Neither do I,' Rory agreed softly. 'Ally, she's tired, she's old and, like you said, she'd hate the fact that she can't even get out to the toilet.'

'Should I ring him now?' Ally asked 'Tell him to just come and…?' Her voice trailed off. She was unable to even think it, let alone say it, and even though she was used to making life-and-death decisions with objectivity and assertiveness, and even though Sheba was only a dog, she was hers; her friend. Sheba had been by her side each and every day during good times and bad, and staring down at those soft velvety eyes, she tried to make the right decision by her friend yet longed to keep her for a little while longer. Ally truly didn't know what to do for the best.

'Maybe let him know,' Rory suggested, 'but she looks pretty comfortable now. The tablet must be starting too kick in and she's got you home. Why don't you ask him to come tomorrow—and have tonight with Sheba?'

'I'm supposed to be working tomorrow,' Ally faltered, as Rory held out the telephone to her, not wanting to make the call.

'There's no way you're going to be able to work tomorrow,' Rory argued. 'Ring and tell them now before you speak to the vet—that will give them plenty of time to get a replacement.'

'And tell them what?' Ally asked. 'That I need a sick day because of my dog?'

'Yes,' Rory said simply. 'When was the last time you took sick leave, Ally?'

She didn't answer. After all, she could hardly tell him that the last time she'd called in sick had been the day he'd left for the States, so instead she rang the ward, and the sympathy and understanding in her colleague's voice only made her choke up even more.

'I've got the day off.' Ally sniffed, hating what she had to do now. Trembling fingers dialed a number and she left a voicemail message asking for Dale to get back to her.

'He must think I'm such a wimp,' Ally said, still on her knees, still stroking Sheba's head. 'I cried my eyes out when I rang him this morning and again when he came to see her.'

'I'm sure he's used to it,' Rory said. 'Do you want me to speak to him for you?' And Ally surprised even herself by nodding.

'Thank you.'

'I'll ask him what we should do if she gets really distressed in the night.'

'Me or the dog?' Ally managed a very feeble

joke as Rory bought her over a mug of coffee and sat down on the floor beside her. 'I already asked him that. He gave me a couple of sedatives for her and said to give her those and a couple more of the painkillers and he'd come straight out.'

'He sounds nice.'

'He is.' Ally sniffed again. 'He's actually an equine vet. He's got that massive horse hospital on the peninsula.'

'And he does house visits for dogs!' Rory said, the surprise evident in his voice, but he quickly checked himself. 'I didn't mean it to come out like that.'

'I know.' Ally smiled. 'He didn't have the hospital when Sheba was a puppy and he kept on a few of his regular clients when he built the equine hospital. Sheba's probably one of the last canines he's got on his list—he's always been great with her.'

They both jumped when the phone rang and Ally was infinitely grateful for Rory's earlier offer, because as soon as the vet introduced himself Ally burst into noisy tears and, not wanting to upset Sheba, had to go and lock herself in the bedroom for a few moments as Rory dealt with the practicalities. She emerged red-eyed and red-nosed to be told what had been decided.

'He's got Theatre early in the morning and he said he'd be here around eleven.'

'Thanks.'

'He said you were doing the right thing.'

Ally gave a small nod.

'Do you want me to carry her into your room for the night?' Rory offered, but Ally shook her head.

'It's too far for her if she wants to get out.'

'Then do you want me to drag a mattress in here? You can sleep beside her, and if she wakes up and wants to go outside, you can call me and I'll carry her out.'

In some ways she wished he'd tell her to pull herself together and remind her that Sheba was just a dog. His insight and kindness was almost more than she could bear.

'Please.' And later on he did just that, made up a bed for Ally on the kitchen floor. Twice in the night without a murmur of complaint, he carried the old dog out into the garden, doing everything he could to make her last few hours as comfortable and as dignified as possible.

Doing everything he could to make things just a little bit more bearable for Ally.

CHAPTER SIX

'WHY don't you ring your mum and ask her to come over?'

Despite a very disturbed night, Rory looked amazingly together—freshly showered and wearing aftershave, he stood in a charcoal grey suit ready for ward rounds. Ally lay on the mattress dressed in flannel pyjamas, surrounded by a pile of crumpled tissues and with red swollen slits for eyes.

'Mum won't be any help,' Ally sniffed. 'She'll be worse than me. I'll be OK.'

'If it wasn't my first week, I'd take the day off.'

'Rory, you don't need to take time off.' Ally managed a grateful smile. 'I think I'm pushing things asking for a day's leave—can you imagine if the obstetric registrar rang in sick as well over a dog!'

'I guess,' Rory sighed. 'But she's kind of more than just a dog, aren't you, girl?' He bent down to stroke a dozing Sheba and Ally swore she saw a flash of tears in his dark green eyes. 'Ring me if you need anything.'

'I won't.' Ally shook her head. 'You've done more than enough.'

She didn't say goodbye and neither did Rory. She just listened as the front door closed quietly and tried to summon the strength to face this horrible day, wanting to somehow make it special for Sheba, to cook her a treat for breakfast perhaps. But all Sheba wanted to do was sleep and, exhausted, Ally did the same, waking with a jolt of horror a few hours later and realising that it was ten o'clock.

It was one of the longest and shortest hours of her life. There was nothing really to do except stroke Sheba's tired head and watch the clock with dry eyes. Even though it was expected, the knock on the door just before eleven had her heart racing.

What wasn't expected was Rory standing beside the vet and his nurse.

'I asked Dale to give me a call when he left the surgery to come here.'

'You didn't have to.' Ally's voice wobbled as she led the vet through to the kitchen, apologising as she did so for the mess.

'I know,' Rory murmured as Dale knelt down and examined the dog. 'I didn't want to say anything in case I couldn't get away.'

'Do you want to be here, Ally?' Dale asked. Words failing her, Ally gave a small nod. 'I think we should go ahead and do this now,' Dale said quietly. 'She isn't going to improve and Rory told me on the phone she'd had an accident yesterday. For a proud old thing like Sheba, that would have been upsetting.'

'Rory's carried her out since then,' Ally said, baulking at the final hurdle. 'And she's been really comfortable all morning. Maybe she will pick up.'

'I don't think so,' Dale said gently. 'And it's kind of nice to do it while she is comfortable, Ally. It would be awful to see the old girl getting distressed or sick.'

'Do it,' Ally sobbed, tears choking her as the nurse shaved a tiny patch of hair on Sheba's leg and Dale filled up a syringe. She couldn't watch what happened, just buried her head in her best friend's old body and hugged her hard, telling her over and over what a great friend she'd been and how lucky Ally had been to have her as a pet. And it was over in a moment. A last lick of Ally's hand as if somehow Sheba was saying thank you too, and with the gentlest of shudders, Ally felt her beautiful pet relax beneath her. She held her fiercely for a moment or two longer before letting her go.

'It's done.' Rory helped her up as Dale and the nurse cleared up the equipment.

'You did the right thing by her,' Dale said.

'She deserved it,' Ally sniffed, curiously dry-eyed now, relieved in a way that it was over. She'd been dreading this day for months now, had felt sick sometimes just thinking about it, but seeing Sheba lying there so peaceful and relaxed Ally felt calm, too. 'Do you want me to take her for you?' Dale offered, and Ally agreed. She rummaged in her bag for her purse, but Dale wouldn't hear of taking a payment for one of his oldest clients.

'Please,' Ally pushed, but he shook his head.

'Why don't you go and wait in the lounge room? We'll let ourselves out.'

Ally did as she was told, walking on legs that felt like jelly through to the lounge and waiting as Rory helped the vet out to his Jeep. She managed a wan smile when he came back in.

'OK?' Rory asked, blowing out a long breath, his hands two fists by his sides, and Ally was touched to see how much this had affected him, too.

'Better than I thought I'd be.'

His pager went off in his pocket and Ally

stood quietly as he picked up the phone and checked his message.

'I'd better get back,' he said, not worrying her with whatever the hospital wanted, knowing she didn't need it now. 'Are you sure you'll be all right?'

'I'll be fine.' Ally nodded. 'Thank you for coming home—that was nice of you.'

'No problem.' He stood across the room and for the first time Ally sensed his awkwardness. His voice was slightly wooden when he spoke. 'Do you want me to take her basket and bowl and things?'

'I'll do that,' Ally answered, her voice equally false.

'I'd better go, then.'

'Sure.'

He turned to leave, but midway changed his mind and crossed the room to where she stood. As he held out his arms she leaned into him. She didn't have to be brave and sensible for that precious moment as he held her shaky, pyjama-clad body. It felt so nice being in his arms, resting in his strong embrace. Closing her eyes, she inhaled his scent, allowed him to comfort her for just a little while, wishing that she could stay there for ever, lean on Rory and let him in close.

'I've got to go.' His voice was thick with emotion, his arms contradicting his words because still he was holding her, making no move to let her go. His mouth rested on the top of her head and he spoke into her hair. The comforting embrace wasn't quite so comforting now, a tiny shift moving it to pleasantly disturbing, his grip tighter as he held her, his hand moving slowly down her hair. It was almost indefinable what was taking place, but it was palpable, the friendship she had insisted on evaporating as he held her for the first time in three long years. Time melted away and Ally was back where she had once thought she would always be, and it would have been the easiest thing to lift her head. Ally knew that if she did so he'd be waiting for her, that his lips would find hers, and she wanted so badly to comfort herself with his kiss, wanted so badly to take this moment and stretch it further, but in a moment of clarity she knew it would be foolish, knew she'd be letting emotion get the better of her. In a regretful jolt of self-preservation she wriggled out of his embrace, forced a small smile and looked into his eyes, trying to pretend that nothing had just happened.

'See you, Rory.' She sounded as if she had a cold, her voice thick from a night spent crying. 'Thanks again for being here.'

'I'll see you tonight,' Rory said, clearing his throat. He was also back in housemate mode, playing the game too, his voice normal now, going through the motions and heading out of the door.

CHAPTER SEVEN

'HI, ALLY.' Hearing the door slam. Ally took a deep breath as Rory made his way down the hall and managed a smile as he walked into the lounge room with a delicious-smelling take-away in a brown paper bag. 'I didn't think that you'd feel much like cooking…' His voice sort of faded out as he noticed that Ally wasn't alone, and nodded a greeting to the two women sitting like bookends either side of Ally on the sofa. 'Oh, hi. Sorry, I didn't realise that you had company. Becky, isn't it?' He smiled at Ally's friend, blonde and bronzed from a fortnight in the Queensland sun and a couple of hundred dollars' worth of highlights at the hairdresser's.

'Hi, Rory.' Becky grinned. 'Long time no see!'

'Yeah, it's been way too long…' His eyes

creased in concentration as he tried to place the other face. 'You're not Donna, are you?'

'I certainly am!'

'My goodness!' Rory smiled in amazement. 'Look at you—or should I say look at what's left of you. You've lost so much weight!'

'Thirty kilos,' Donna said proudly, then rolled her eyes. 'It was sheer bloody hell.'

'Well, you look fantastic. It's good to see you both.' He looked at Ally and she squirmed under his scrutiny—suddenly acutely aware of her unbrushed hair and swollen red face and horribly embarrassed to still be dressed in her pyjamas. But between Sheba being put down and frantic phone calls to her two best friends, it hadn't even entered her head to shower and get dressed.

'How are you bearing up?'

'I'm good. We're just about to watch a DVD.' Ally answered, watching as his gaze moved to the two bottles of wine opened on the coffee-table. 'That wasn't all me!'

'I don't care if it was,' Rory said. 'I was just thinking I could murder one.'

'Here,' Donna offered, pouring him a very generous glass and shooting Ally a frantic look. 'What food did you bring? It smells wonderful.'

'Just noodles,' Rory answered, 'But there should be enough for four of us.' He held up the take-away. 'Or I could always go and pick up some more.'

'Sounds lovely...' Donna winced as Ally kicked her on the ankle.

'Oh, sorry, Rory.' Ally delivered the apologetic shrug she'd been rehearsing for the last half-hour or so. 'I didn't realise you'd be bringing back food. We've already eaten.'

'No problem,' Rory said. 'I'll go and get changed and then I'll have this in the kitchen and leave you to your film.' He raised an eyebrow as he picked up the DVD cover. 'That's not going to cheer you up, you know—you always bawl your eyes out at this one.'

'I don't want to be cheered up,' Ally said. 'You're welcome to watch it with us.'

'We can paint your toenails for you,' Donna

offered, holding up her makeup bag. With a smile Rory shook his head just as Ally had known he would. Rory would never invade what was clearly a girls' night in.

'No, thanks, ladies, I'll leave you to it. I'll bring in some tissues for you all later!'

'There's none left.' Ally held up the loo roll she was holding and forced a smile as Rory closed the door behind him.

'That was so mean,' Donna wailed, once the door was safely shut and the volume on the television was turned up loud.

'It was what we planned,' Becky snapped, 'until you nearly went and blew it. The reason we're here is so that Ally can *avoid* being with him, and one sniff of noodles and you're asking him to join us!'

'It wasn't the noodles,' Donna said huffily. 'I'd forgotten how lovely he was, and it just seems so unfair to leave him sitting alone in the kitchen…'

Ally listened to her two friends bickering, but her mind was on Rory, wondering if she had been a bit callous. After all he'd been so kind to her today. But that was the nature of sharing a house, Ally reminded herself. You made yourself scarce when your housemate had friends over, and she was allowed to have friends over, for goodness' sake. Surely he didn't think she'd spent the last three years sitting with Sheba and pining for him each night!

Almost as soon as Rory had left after Sheba had died, Ally had been trying to get hold of Donna and Becky, praying that she'd got their flight times right and that they'd be home soon. She'd begged them to come over as soon as they picked up the phone—a jumbled, frantic call, where she'd somehow told them about Sheba and Rory coming back, and that he'd given her a cuddle in the hall and that what had started as cuddle had suddenly changed even though *nothing had happened.* And, as friends so easily did, they had zipped over in record time and planted themselves on her sofa. Reinforcements had arrived just when needed, and together they'd planned Ally's defence if Rory decided to attack!

'Anyway,' Donna said, 'why would it be so terrible if you two did get it together?'

'Do you remember the state she was in last time?' Becky answered for Ally.

'I wasn't *that* bad,' Ally bristled, but Becky gave her a wide-eyed look that said she clearly thought otherwise.

'I was more upset at how he'd used me than the fact he'd gone to the States!'

She looked to Donna for support but Donna's expression was equally disbelieving. 'Maybe he's changed,' she suggested hopefully. 'After all, you said that he hasn't been out with anyone since he's been back.'

'It's only Wednesday,' Becky pointed out with a dry smile. 'Look, *if* he has changed and *if* he really does like Ally, then a couple of weeks aren't going to make a difference, are they?' Ally shook her head glumly. 'So all you have to do is avoid being alone with him for a couple of weeks.'

'We live together,' Ally pointed out.

'Well, stop cuddling up to him in the lounge like you did this morning,' Becky said, a touch too harshly. 'All you have to do is avoid physical contact—if you don't touch him, you can't sleep with him! It's like being an alcoholic—if you don't have one drink, you can't have ten.'

'So I'm addicted to Rory Donovan, am I?' Ally muttered. 'Hell, Becky, it's not as if we walk around the place holding hands. I don't think there actually is any physical contact—well, apart from this afternoon.'

'Just think about it,' Becky insisted. 'If you're in the lounge, make sure you sit on one of the chairs, he's hardly able to perch on one of the edges—that type of thing. It'll work, you'll see!'

'Thanks for the advice,' Ally muttered, but she'd lost her audience now. Becky and Donna had turned their attention to the film, and even though it was as sad as she remembered, even though it had been an emotionally draining day, for some reason Ally couldn't even squeeze out a tear. She just stared dry-eyed at the screen and peeled off pieces of loo paper as her two friends sobbed beside her. She even managed a tiny eye roll as Rory waved the tearful pair off from the kitchen when the film was over and they said good-night.

'Did you enjoy the movie?' Rory asked. He was dressed in shorts and a T-shirt now, eating cereal straight out of the box and reading the newspaper—nothing like the suited sophisticated guy who had appeared at the door a couple of hours before, but twice as gorgeous somehow. 'Well, as much as one can enjoy that type of thing!'

'I had a nice evening.' Ally gave a tired smile and, mindful of her friends' advice, smothered a fake yawn. 'But I'm tired now. I think I might go to bed.'

'I just ran you a bath.' Rory grinned at her rather startled expression. 'I thought you could use it to relax. Isn't that what you're always telling your mums to be—that a nice deep bath helps you to unwind?'

'I guess.' Ally blinked—

'And I figured it might be time to get out of those pyjamas.'

'I *was* intending to have a shower,' Ally said, padding along the hallway to the bathroom, forgetting to even say thank you because this wasn't what she'd intended at all. Peeling off her pyjamas, Ally sank into the deep warm bath—he'd even added a squirt of shampoo to give her bubbles. But far from relaxing her, Ally felt more tense than she had all evening! A quick goodnight was what she'd been planning, followed by a long shower in her en suite and no reason to see Rory at all. But this way she'd have to go back through the kitchen. A wave of horror washed over her as she realised she hadn't bought a change of clothes, that she'd have to wander through the house wrapped in a towel.

As if he'd even notice, Ally consoled herself. Becky had no idea what she was talking about.

Anyway, if she stayed in long enough, surely he'd go to bed. But an hour later, shrivelled like a prune and freezing in the tepid water, Ally had to admit defeat. Wrapping a massive towel around her shivering body, she tentatively made her way through the kitchen where Rory was still sitting immersed in the newspaper. She walked in a wide circle around the kitchen table as if he had leprosy, and almost jumped out of her skin when he spoke to her.

'Better?' Rory looked up from the newspaper and, pulling the towel tighter around her, Ally gave a nod. 'Do you want a warm drink?' He pulled out the chair next to him and he might just as well have pulled out a knife as Ally jumped backwards, clutching the towel around her body. 'Hey! Relax, Ally, you're really tense!'

'I'm fine, Rory. I'm not an invalid—I don't need you to baby me.'

'I know.' He gave her a worried smile. 'I just wanted to make sure you were OK. Well, if you don't want a drink or a chat, then I guess I'll head off to bed. 'Night, then.'

''Night, Rory,' Ally said. 'Thanks for everything today.'

'No problem.'

Needlessly she stood back as he passed, kept her brittle smile in place as he headed down the hall towards his room. Proud of herself, Ally let out the breath she'd inadvertently been holding and went to go to bed herself.

''Night, Sheba.' She said it without thinking and turned to where Sheba's basket should have been. Seeing the empty space, missing the sound of Sheba's tail thumping against the wicker, every last piece of bravado crumpled. She broke into noisy sobs and Rory did a prompt about-turn, his face resigned as he found her in hysterics in the kitchen. Becky would have gone mad if she'd seen her, wrapped only in a towel in the kitchen, sobbing into his T-shirt as Rory moved her away from the offending empty space where Sheba had slept.

'Maybe a bottle of wine and a tragic movie wasn't the best idea,' he said, gently teasing her as he frogmarched her down the hall to her bedroom.

'I only had two glasses,' Ally gulped, sitting lamely on the edge of the bed as Rory pulled out one of her oversize T-shirts and turned his back as Ally obediently put it on.

'Bed,' Rory said, pulling back the duvet and ordering her inside. Ally attempted elegant as she climbed into bed, but it was hard, wearing a T-shirt with no knickers and a six-foot-seven mountain of testosterone watching your every move. Pulling the duvet up to her neck, Ally couldn't even bring herself to look at him as Rory attempted a gentle scold. 'You've done enough crying for today, and you're on an early shift tomorrow, so you're not to lie there crying all night. I want you to close your eyes and go to sleep.'

'I'll try,' Ally said, dutifully closing her eyes and biting hard on her bottom lip as Rory flicked off the light. She wished he'd just go, but somehow she also wanted him to stay. Maybe he read her mind because, instead of leaving her, she felt the indentation of the bed as he sat down on the edge. Her hand curled into a tight, unyielding ball as he wrapped his much larger one around hers, massaging her fingers slowly until finally she relaxed a bit. Her fingers uncurled and laced into his and she let him comfort her. But only as a friend would, Ally assured herself, trying to pretend that it was Donna or even Becky helping her through this horrible first night without Sheba.

'I'll let you sleep.' As Ally pulled her hand away, she felt the mattress lift as Rory stood, missing the quiet warmth of him before he'd even left the room.

'Don't go.' The words were out before she had time to mentally process them, a completely instinctive reflex action, and she shuddered at her own boldness, questioned the wisdom of asking him to stay even as he sat down again on the bed beside her.

'Do you want me to lie with you?' Rory offered. 'Just on top of the bed?'

It was the sort of thing that Becky or Donna would have done, given that Sheba had just died, but Ally couldn't fool herself that it was Becky or Donna sitting on the bed next to her and she certainly couldn't if he lay down beside her.

'No.' She shook her head on the pillow, silent tears squeezing out of her closed eyes and rolling into her hair as she fought with a hundred and one conflicting emotions.

'I can't just sit here,' Rory said ages later, when it was clear that she wasn't going to sleep. 'I've got to be up early tomorrow, Ally. I can either go to bed or lie down here—it's up to you.'

'If you lie down,' Ally sniffed, 'then we'll end up sleeping together and you'll walk out in the morning.'

She could feel him smiling in the darkness at her honesty, and felt his hand squeeze tighter around hers as he struggled to respond to her very direct logic.

'We'll sleep together,' Rory said in his deep low voice, 'but not in that way, and the only place I'm going in the morning is work.'

And that sounded enough of a guarantee, sounded pretty safe, and she wriggled over an inch as he lay down on the bed beside her, lifted her head a touch as he slipped a strong arm underneath her and pulled her closer towards him.

'You've had a rotten day,' Rory murmured into the darkness, 'but it's over now. Try thinking of something nice.'

Which wasn't hard! Lying beside him, feeling the steady sound of his breathing, Ally felt for the first time in ages that she was where she belonged. She could feel the dusting sensation of the little hairs on his arm against her neck, the heavy masculine scent of him, and it was easy, way too easy to curl into him, to rest her head on his chest and feel the slow beat of his heart. Her arm moved across his flat stomach, the darkness making her bold. The sensual shift that had taken place earlier in the living room had never really gone away, but it was creeping back into her awareness. She knew he felt it, too, could hear the slight quickening of his breath, the tension flooding the very body Ally was relaxing into.

'Maybe I should go and let you rest.' His words were austere and formal, his hand wrapped around her wrist and firmly moved it away from where it rested. Ally resisted his movement, tensed in his arms as he gently tried to move her away.

'Ally, maybe this wasn't such a good idea after all. I don't think I can just lie here…'

'Then don't,' Ally said, but there was a pro-vocative undertone to her voice that made it clear that she wasn't asking him to leave, but asking him to stay, and as she lay there beside him she felt the tension of denial seeping out of him. He accepted her touch more naturally now as she eased her body back into his. The hand that had lain rigid beside her was stroking her hair now. They were just lying in each other's arms and enjoying the peace of being together, of acknowledging the attraction Ally had been furiously denying. His caress was gentle but intimate, and maybe it was the most stupid decision of her life, maybe she'd live to regret it, but if the last few days had taught Ally one thing, it had shown her that it was impossible for her to just be friends with Rory, impossible to just have a little piece of him instead of all. And if they couldn't work it out as lovers, they couldn't work it out as friends either. Ally knew that living in the same house, working alongside him each day and holding her feelings deep inside had turned out to be an impossible task—and if losing all of him was the price she'd have to pay somewhere down the line for her honesty, if laying herself open to possible hurt was the risk, then Ally was prepared to accept it. But Rory needed to be sure. Propping himself up on his elbow and staring down at her, tracing her cheekbones with his finger, staring into her eyes with the intimate gaze of a lover, he said, 'Ally, I don't want you to regret anything tomorrow…'

'Then don't hurt me again,' Ally said, and stared at him in the darkness. Her words simple but honest, she watched as he closed his eyes in regret.

'I never intended to hurt you, Ally. I just didn't see how it could work. I didn't want to lose our friendship…'

'You nearly did,' Ally said softly. 'I couldn't go through it again, Rory. Couldn't be friends if you pushed me away again.' Despite the intimacy, despite the gentleness of her words, there was a tiny warning ring to them. As he pulled her fiercely into his arms Ally knew that he had heeded it, knew as his lips searched for hers that he was affirming he understood, that if they crossed the line now there could be no going back, no pretending feelings hadn't been hurt, for Ally could never forgive him twice.

His kiss was worth the wait, worth the pain, the familiar taste of him as he pressed his flesh against hers causing tiny ripples of pleasure to course through her, feeling his breath mingling with hers, just parting long enough for him to undress her. He slipped the T-shirt over her head as she lifted her arms and she was naked beside him, deliciously exposed. The desire in his eyes, the utter adoration that blazed from them as he gazed the length of her body told her she was beautiful enough for audacity, made her bold enough to undress him, to pull at the T-shirt and expose the flesh she had craved for so long, to tug at his boxers and reveal the man who had guiltily invaded her dreams for three long years now. And her memory hadn't done him justice. His body was more beautiful than she'd even allowed herself to remember, but there was a thrill of familiarity as tentative fingers dusted the dark hairs of his chest, felt the solid muscle beneath her touch. And her lips could only relish him, taste the salty velvet of his skin. Her desire was overwhelming now as Rory took control, took her slender body in his arms, his lips, his tongue exploring her, tasting her, savouring her. The ecstasy of being held by someone as strong and as male as Rory was one of life's all-time pleasures that reared again as if it had never been buried. His maleness only enhanced her femininity and she revelled in it, enjoying the comparative fragility of her own body as his hands tenderly explored it, fingers tracing the long slender length of her spine, his lips, his tongue working the shadows of her neck along her shoulder and her legs wrapped around his. His size was only rivalled by his tenderness. 'Oh, Ally,' he murmured over and over into her hair.

And she answered him with her body, arching herself towards him, and it couldn't be too quick or too soon when she'd waited for him so long. She was so warm and inviting and ready, so eager for him to take her that as he slipped inside her needy warmth, loved her as only Rory ever could. It was Ally who lost control first, feeling the swell of him inside her, his athletic frame hovering over her as he glided deep within, her legs dragging him in deeper, harder, and she knew he didn't want to hurt her, but she also knew that he couldn't. The passion was overriding now as he rocked deep within her, her fingers digging into his shoulders, her pelvis tipping into his, and it was Ally attempting to cry out his name as he filled her. Her orgasm was so intense that even speech failed her. Her whole body shuddered as he shivered deep inside her, the last throes of her orgasm so intense her eyes shot open and she stared deep into his, the moment so intimate, so tender she needed to see him, needed to hold his gaze as she surrendered. They needed to witness this together.

'Do you have any idea how much I've missed you?' It was Rory who spoke first, Rory pulling her out of her delicious post-coital stupor and into beautiful reality.

'No.' Lying in his arms, she shook her head against his chest, felt the weight of his lips as he kissed the top of her head. Cocooned in love, all she wanted to do was sleep, to lie in Rory's arms and wait for tomorrow, wait to experience the one thing that so far they hadn't.

CHAPTER EIGHT

'MORNING.' Green eyes were welcoming her, tiny lines fanning at the sides of his eyes as he welcomed her to a new day, a new life with Rory by her side. The one thing that had been missing from her dreams finally materialised—no suitcase in the hall, no air ticket on the dresser, no hasty exit before she woke up, just Rory in bed beside her. And it was like saying goodbye to a recurring nightmare and slipping into a dream.

'You're still here?'

'Still here,' Rory said. 'Feel.'

So she did, but not where he'd intended, and Rory was as taken aback as he was delighted by her boldness. Their hazy, languorous, early morning love-making was like a delicious second course—appetites quenched by the entrée and more time now to relish the main course, bodies warm and relaxed from a night in each other's arms, the rumpled bed…

'Sorry.' Reaching out for his pager, Rory squinted at the offending item, before picking up the phone and dialling the hospital. Realising he was probably going to be called in, Ally went to get out of bed to make coffee, but Rory caught her wrist and pulled her back as he concluded the conversation and put down the phone.

'I'm expecting twins!'

'Congratulations.' Ally grinned—pinching his line. 'I'll go and make some coffee while you have a shower.'

'Rinska's there.' Rory pulled her back down beside him. 'And there's a long way to go yet. Now, where were we?'

Thankfully the maternity unit was impossibly busy when Ally arrived for her shift—thankfully, because it kept people from asking why someone who should be so depressed was hard pushed to keep the smile from her face.

Win waylaid her the second she arrived, her lined face filled with concern. 'How are you, love? Jess told me that poor old Sheba wasn't well and that you had to have her put down.'

'I did.' Ally blew her fringe into the air, wondering how one could feel so deliriously happy and so sad at the same time. 'But it wasn't as bad as I thought it would be. She was so old, I knew it had to be done and the vet was terribly kind—everyone's been great really. How are you doing, Win?'

'I'm not sure,' Win admitted. 'I feel a bit like Sheba myself—everyone's being terribly kind, but I know they think I'm too old for the place. My supervisor's asked to talk with me at ten this morning. No doubt I'm about to get my marching orders.'

'They can't just sack you.'

'No, but apparently they can send me down to A and E. I've been really pushing myself to do the forty-hour weeks because I don't want to let the job go, and then yesterday I got a call telling me to go down to the accident unit and help out after my lunch-break. In thirty years I've never left this ward.'

'Did you go?' Ally asked, looking at Win's tired, worried face and wishing she could do something more to help.

'No.' Win shook her head. 'Dr Rory told me to stay put and went down and spoke to the supervisor himself. No doubt that's why I'm being called in for a little *chat* this morning. I know he meant well, but he's not the one who's going to cop it today.'

'Good luck.' Ally gave a sympathetic grimace, wishing there was more she could say. 'Let me know how you get on.'

'How are you feeling?' Jess asked, making a space for Ally as she came in to take the handover.

'Better,' Ally admitted. 'I was just saying to Win that I was a wreck yesterday, but to tell you the truth, I've been dreading it for so long now, once it happened it was almost a relief.

I'm going to miss her like crazy but I really think she was kind of holding on just to keep me happy. I know it was her time.'

'You'll still have your moments,' Jess warned, and Ally nodded, her nose reddening as she did just that—thought about Sheba who'd patiently listened to each and every instalment of Ally's love life, only to miss out on the final episode.

Maybe she knew, Ally consoled herself, clicking on her pen as handover started. Maybe once Rory had come back, Sheba had somehow felt she could leave.

'Ally, Jess.' Vivien looked over at the two women. 'If you can cover delivery, please. It's pretty full on in there this morning so take the student Marcus with you. There are three women labouring at the moment and one set of identical twins about to be delivered—I think Marcus should see that. We've also had a call from Fiona Anderson. She's in first-stage labour and is making her way in to us shortly.'

'Finally!' Ally grinned. 'How are we for beds?'

'A bit tight,' Vivien replied. 'Though there should be a few discharges this morning and hopefully we won't get too many more in, but if we do, we're just going to have to shuffle.'

'Twins!' Ally beamed, heading over to the delivery unit with Jess and Marcus and taking a more detailed handover from the midwife in charge. They introduced themselves to the patients and relatives, and read through the patients' charts that mapped out the progress of each woman's labour.

As they arrived in Louise Williams's room it was a scene of quiet activity. Rinska was performing the delivery as Rory supervised closely. They were already gowned up and completely focused on the task in hand and Ally neither expected nor received a smile from the man who had left her bed that morning. She wouldn't have had it any other way—the patient and her precious babies rightly demanded all his attention. The paediatrician was pulling up various drugs by one of the two cots that were being warmed on the other side of the delivery room as an anaesthetist stood by. Even though, with the rise in IVF babies, twins were becoming a more regular occurrence, they still carried a higher risk of complications, hence the increase in staff for this delivery. Louise's double miracle had nothing to do with *in vitro* fertilization though—identical twins were a natural and sporadic phenomenon and also very exciting!

'I might hang around for this one.' Bella, the night midwife, smiled. 'Louise has been an absolute delight and she's so close now. The second baby is breech…'

'Breech!' Marcus said, startled by the information, but Bella gave a reassuring smile. 'The second baby often is with twins, but it normally doesn't cause a problem. It will be nice for you to see an easy breech birth and get to grips with the mechanics before you have to witness a more difficult one. Anyway, we've got Rory and Rinska in here so I'm sure it's all going to go well. I'll go and see how Mum's doing.'

Jess went off to check the equipment and help the paediatrician and anaesthetist, leaving Ally with a nervous Marcus.

'Identification is especially important with twins, and particularly when they're identical,' Ally said, showing Marcus the two neat sets of charts labelled twin one and twin two. 'These name tags will have been checked with Mum and as soon as the first baby is born the baby will have a name tag put on.'

'They always do,' Marcus said.

'Before the cord's cut in this case,' Ally said to her student. 'There may well be a distinguishing feature—one might just be bigger than the other—but there's nothing worse that mixing up babies.' Opening a small container, Ally smiled as Marcus frowned at the contents.

'Nail varnish?'

'Cherry-red nail varnish,' Ally corrected. 'Each hospital has their own methods, but here we paint the first baby's big toe with nail varnish, with the mum's consent, of course. There's no chance of it slipping off, as name tags sometimes do, and this will last for days, weeks even, giving Mum plenty of time to be able to tell her twins apart without panicking that she's mixed them up.'

'Does that really happen?' Marcus asked dubiously. 'I read that the mother can always tell which one's which.'

'That's what the books say.' Ally smiled. 'And, yes, normally Mum can soon tell them apart. But what the books don't take into account is that at five a.m. after an exhausting night up with her babies and in a darkened room, she may well get confused. This way she can relax a bit. Remember that Mum's hopefully going to have a stream of relatives lining up to help with feeds and changes and this way all they have to do is check a toe to know which one they just fed and changed. It helps the staff, too!'

'It makes sense,' Marcus agreed, warming to the logic.

'Ally.' One of the night staff, on her way home, popped her head around the door and, yawning, said, 'Fiona Anderson's just arrived.'

'Thanks.' Thrilled that Fiona was here and keen to be a part of her labour, Ally also felt reluctance to leave this imminent delivery, but as Jess was in the thick of things now and Bella had already offered to stay on for the birth, Ally had no choice but to go.

'Morning, Fiona. Morning, Mark. You're finally here!'

'Finally,' Fiona groaned, leaning up against the wall as another contraction took over. Ally waited patiently, unobtrusively timing the contraction with the clock on the wall and gently placing her hand on Fiona's stomach to feel how strong it was.

'How far apart are they?' Ally asked when Fiona straightened up again. 'They feel pretty strong.'

'They are,' Fiona agreed, 'and they're coming every four or five minutes. I thought

I'd want to be at home for ages, but when the pain really kicked in the only place I wanted to be was here.'

Sometimes women in early labour, especially first-time mums, were kept on the ward until their labour was rather more advanced, but, given the closeness of the contractions and the fact that the ward was pretty full, Ally guided Fiona through to one of the vacant delivery suites, showing her the bathroom and the various switches and gadgets that she would soon be familiar with.

'This is a nice room—with views!' Fiona added, taking in the gorgeous ocean view.

'Amazing, isn't it?' Ally smiled. 'And something nice and calming to focus on when you're having a contraction. If it gets too bright we can pull the curtains. I'm just going to have a quick listen to the baby's heartbeat if I may,' Ally said. 'This is called a Doppler.'

'I saw that in class.' Fiona nodded, lifting up her T-shirt as Ally squirted some cold jelly on her stomach and quickly picked up the reassuring sounds of the baby's heartbeat.

'Nice and regular,' Ally said. 'I'll check it more thoroughly once you're undressed, but for now everything sounds fine. Now, this is the call bell—use it whenever you want. If it isn't urgent, just press it once and we'll get to you just as soon as we can—we've got quite a few mums labouring at the moment so we're pretty busy.'

'It sounds it!' Fiona winced as a rather ear-splitting scream filled the entire delivery unit. Then Ally watched as Fiona's terrified face broke into a smile as, just seconds later, the lusty sounds of a newborn filled the room. 'Is that a baby just been born?'

'It is.' Ally nodded, and even though she was completely calm and her face gave nothing away, Ally was on high alert now, hoping that twin two would do just as well, mindful that it was a breech delivery and that at any moment she could be summoned to assist. With one ear on suite one and the other on her new patient, Ally multi-tasked as easily as breathing. 'Like I said, just press it once, but if you need someone quickly, you or Mark are to press it three times and we'll come straight away.'

'Got it,' Fiona said, bending over as another contraction hit.

Ally glanced back up at the clock wall. 'They're pretty close together.' Ally gave a smile and encouraged her patient to breathe through the pain, reminding her of the methods she'd taught her in class. 'That's the way,' Ally said in gentle voice. 'Breathe out slowly—you're doing so well.' Once the contraction was over Ally dealt with the practicalities. 'Why don't you get into something more comfortable and then I'll come and check on you and the baby and see how you're both doing? Are you wearing your own clothes or would you like a hospital gown?'

'A gown, please.'

'Good choice,' Ally agreed, pulling a gown out of the cupboard and handing it to Mark.

'OK, if you give Fiona a hand to get changed, I'll go and grab all the notes and paperwork and we can get things moving for you.' She pulled a rocking chair out from the wall and turned it towards the window. 'Do you remember how I said in class that rocking often helps…?' Her voice trailed off for a moment as twin one's cries were joined by twin two's and Ally let out a small relieved breath.

'Twins,' she explained as Fiona frowned, but it wasn't the fact that it was two babies crying that was concerning Fiona. Instead, it was the fact that another contraction was starting. She lowered herself into the chair, rocking tentatively at first and then picking up speed as the pain intensified. Ally stood quietly, watching Fiona's closed eyes, not wanting to interrupt her.

'That helps!' Fiona blinked in surprise. 'That really helps!'

'Enjoy!' Ally said, leaving her patient to get into a gown. But instead of heading straight to the cupboard to collect the paperwork, she popped into delivery suite one, where the sound of two lusty cries was filling the air.

'Boys.' Jess beamed. 'And they're absolutely gorgeous.'

'Oh, my goodness.' Ally blinked. Clearly they were doing well, because the paediatrician and anaesthetist had already gone and the newborns were wrapped in two bunny rugs and had been placed side by side in just one of the heated cots as Rory delivered the single placenta that had nourished them through the pregnancy. Facing each other, their two blond heads were touching. 'They're like two peas in a pod.'

'Did you ever see anything more divine?' Jess asked and it was Rory who answered as he and Rinska came over to admire the babies.

'No,' Rory said. 'They would have to be two of the cutest babies I've ever seen—and that's saying something.'

He wasn't exaggerating. They were absolutely divine, but, as much as she wanted to stand and gaze for a little longer, that wasn't what Ally was in here for.

'Could one of you come and see my new admission, sooner rather than later? I haven't examined her yet, but the contractions are pretty close and I've a feeling she may well be the next one to deliver. I just don't want to put her through two examinations if I can help it.'

'Sure.' Rinska nodded, tearing her eyes away as Jess and Bella picked up the twins to take them over to Mum for a very well-deserved cuddle. 'I'll be right there—just need to write up Louise's notes.'

Fiona was in a gown by the time Ally returned, and she guided her onto the delivery bed, checking her patient's baseline observations before turning her attention to the baby. Feeling Fiona's stomach, Ally attempted to locate the baby's position, determinedly not showing her worry as the normally easy examination proved rather difficult.

'Is everything OK?' Fiona asked anxiously as Ally gently probed her abdomen.

'I'm just checking the baby's position,' Ally

explained. 'It seems to have moved a bit since the last time you were examined. When did you last have an ultrasound?'

'I only had the one at nineteen weeks,' Fiona answered. 'We didn't want to have too many procedures.'

'OK.' Ally nodded. 'I'm going to strap the CTG machine on now. All it does is record baby's heartbeat and the timing and strength of your contractions so we can see how you and babe are both doing. Have you had a lot of movement?'

'Lots,' Fiona admitted. 'I feel as if it's doing cartwheels inside me sometimes.'

Fiona could well be right, Ally thought as she left Fiona and found Rinska. 'I'm not too sure about this baby's position,' Ally said. 'I think it could be transverse.'

'I'll come now,' Rinska said, leaving the notes she was busily writing. Transverse meant that the baby was lying on its side, and if Ally was right in her assessment, Fiona was going to need some assistance.

Rinska was incredibly gentle as she examined Fiona's stomach. 'Have you done an internal?'

'Not yet.' Ally shook her head, holding her patient's hands as Rinska gently performed the procedure.

'What's the problem?' Fiona's voice was more anxious now and Ally listened as Rinska gently explained her findings.

'Your cervix is dilating nicely and your contractions are strong and regular. However, the baby is in a difficult position.'

'Breech?' Fiona asked, but didn't wait for a reply. 'Because if it is, I want to deliver normally. I've read up on breech births.'

'The baby isn't breech.' Rinska shook her head. 'At least, I don't think so. We'll need an ultrasound to confirm the position, but I think that your baby is lying across your stomach.'

Ally attempted to explain things further as Rinska again palpated the uterus.

'You know how I explained that babies are generally head down for birth? Well, as

Rinska said, it would seem that your baby might be lying in a position that we call transverse…'

'But can I still have a normal delivery?' Fiona pushed, a vaginal birth the only thing on her mind now.

'Let's get the ultrasound machine in,' Rinska said, 'and I'll ask Dr Donovan to come and take a look at you. Once we know exactly how the baby is lying, we'll be able to explore your options, but for now all we would be doing is guessing.' Rinska gave a firm nod. 'Let's wait till we have all the facts. I'll go and get the ultrasound machine…' She paused for a moment as Fiona had another contraction, and came over as she saw Ally's concerned face as she read the CTG tracing.

'I'll go and get Dr Donovan,' Rinska said in a low tone, reluctant to press the bell three times and alarm Fiona with half the ward staff arriving. 'Put her on oxygen.'

Ally was already onto it. The baby had suddenly started to struggle, its erratic heartbeat showing signs of foetal distress, and Ally focused on keeping her patient calm, instructing her to lie on her side to allow for more effective oxygenation of the baby and placing a mask over Fiona's terrified face.

'Fiona.' Ally's voice was calm as her patient panicked. 'The baby's starting to struggle a bit so I want you to take some nice slow deep breaths of the oxygen. I'm just going to put a little needle into the back of your hand in case we need to give you any drugs.'

'I don't want any drugs,' Fiona insisted, but Ally carried on with the task, wrapping a tourniquet around her patient's wrist and swabbing the back of her hand as Rory arrived.

'Hi, Fiona.' Rory smiled down at his patient as he introduced himself. He had the CTG tracing Rinska had ripped off in his hand, and after the briefest of examinations he pulled over a stool and squirted jelly on Fiona's stomach, carefully checking the position of the babe with ultrasound. Every movement was controlled, his voice supremely calm as he spoke with his patient, but though Fiona probably couldn't see it, Ally knew Rory well enough to know he was deeply concerned. The tiny creases around his eyes were deep grooves now, his mouth set in a grim line as he scanned the screen in front of him.

'Fiona.' He looked up at her anxious husband. 'Mark, is it?' Ally listened as he delivered his findings directly to the patient and her partner, her mind racing ahead, pressing on the call bell three times as Rory spoke calmly. 'Your baby is transverse—has that been explained to you?'

'Sort of,' Fiona gulped.

'Well, your baby is actually back down— which makes it a very difficult transverse position. If you imagine your uterus as a cup, your baby is lying across it, with its back at the bottom.' He drew an extremely rudimentary picture but it was enough for Fiona and Mark right now. 'In this position, a vaginal delivery isn't possible.'

As the door opened Ally greeted Jess, giving out her rapid instructions. 'Tell Theatre we're coming—transverse lie, foetal distress...' That was all she needed to say, knowing those words were enough to set the emergency wheels in motion. In a matter of moments the Theatre would be ready, and even by the time Ally had returned to the bedside she could hear the overhead chimes summoning the anaesthetist and the paediatrician to the delivery theatre.'

'You could try turning it...' Fiona was sobbing, her eyes turning to Ally's, pleading with her to support her in her quest to have a natural birth. 'Ally said something about an external version...'

'Not in this case.' Rory shot an angry look at Ally before continuing. 'External version sometimes works, but it can only be attempted if we're happy with the cord position and if the baby is stable. Right now your baby is in distress.' Rory let the words sink in. 'We have to go ahead and perform an urgent Caesarean section so that your baby can receive adequate oxygenation. At the moment it's struggling. I need you to sign a consent form…'

'Well, can I have an epidural?' Fiona begged. 'I want to be awake, I *have* to be awake for this.'

Ally's heart went out to her. Fiona's worst nightmare was ensuing, but every word Rory said was true—this baby had to be born and soon or the consequences would be dire. Thankfully Mark seemed to understand the gravity of the situation.

'Listen to the doctor, Fiona,' he interrupted her tirade. 'Sign the consent form and let the doctors look after our baby!'

Thankfully Mark's words hit home and Fiona's shaky pale hand signed the consent form.

'Good girl.' Rory nodded. 'Fiona, I'm going to go to Theatre now and get scrubbed. I'll see you in there.'

Ally moved the drips and oxygen connections to enable the bed to be wheeled directly into Theatre.

'Go ahead, Ally.' Jess was taking the brakes off the bed. 'I'll wheel Fiona down and you can get ready to receive the babe. You'll see Fiona in Theatre and when I come back I'll talk to you, Mark.'

Ally gave Fiona a quick reassuring squeeze of her hand. 'I'll meet you in Theatre.' Racing down the corridor and into the theatre changing room, Ally quickly pulled off her uniform and dressed in theatre blues, slipping her feet into white clogs and putting on the purple flowered paper cap. Different caps were worn by each staff member to identify them—the scrub nurses' would be blue, Rory's would be green. Making her way into Theatre, Ally was instantly soothed by the ordered efficiency of the place. Already the anaesthetist was pulling up his drugs as the nurses pulled open packs and started the routine check of their equipment. Rory had finished scrubbing and was putting his hands into a gown. Over his mask his eyes met hers, and despite the mask Ally knew from his grim expression that he wasn't smiling behind it.

'Don't,' he said, coming as close as he could without disturbing his sterile field, 'ever do that again.'

'Do what?' Ally blinked, fixing her own mask now and frowning at his hostile voice.

'Don't ever confuse one of my patients like that again. Just because you're so bloody obsessed with natural birth, please, don't pass it on to the patients. You knew how little time we had, and instead of getting on with the job I had to stand there explaining why we can't perform an external version while her baby's heart rate's dropping by the second!'

Oh, she'd have loved to have let him have it! Would have loved to have broken his sterile field and marched right up to him with a smart retort, but the theatre doors were opening now and Fiona was being rushed inside, so for now Ally had to settle for a single sentence.

'Don't—' Ally glowered '—ever judge me without knowing all the facts!'

* * *

'It's OK, Fiona.' Ally held her patient's hand as she was moved swiftly onto the theatre table. Time was of the essence. Fiona's abdomen was prepped with solution and she was attached to noisy bleeping monitors as she lay wide-eyed and terrified. Ally knew it was her job to comfort her patient, to be the one familiar face that Fiona could focus on as she gently explained what was going to happen.

'The anaesthetist is just getting things ready, and once you're attached to all the monitors, he'll put a mask over your face and put you to sleep. We're going to have your baby out in just a moment. Everything's under control.'

'I'm scared!' Fiona wasn't crying now. Her face was as pale as the paper hat she was wearing. 'Is the baby OK?'

'Its heartrate's slow,' Ally said, glancing over to the monitor and keeping her face impassive, 'but Rory will have it delivered in no time…'

'It's a boy.' Fiona bit down on her lip for a

second before continuing. 'Mark doesn't know, he doesn't even know I know, but I sneaked a quick word with the lady who did the ultrasound—I'm going to have a son!'

'In just a couple of minutes,' Ally smiled, holding Fiona's hand as the mask was placed over her face. 'You just think about meeting your son.'

She only let go of Fiona's hand when she was well and truly under. The anaesthetist injected powerful drugs that rendered her unconscious and a tube was placed down her throat so the ventilator did the breathing for her. Ally slipped over to the cot warmer and joined the paediatrician, ensuring they had everything ready.

'Come on, come on.' Hugh, the paediatrician, glanced anxiously at the theatre clock. 'Let's get this baby out.'

'Nearly there.' Rory's voice was tense but controlled, and Ally listened to the gurgling sound as he suctioned out the amniotic fluid. She picked up a sterile green drape to receive the infant when Rory handed it to her, knowing that now he was in, the baby would be here in a matter of seconds.

'Here's the head.' She could see Rory's wide shoulders, shifted herself just enough to watch the grey head emerging, chewing anxiously on her lips behind her mask as the flaccid body was delivered.

'We've got a problem here, Rory.' It was a voice no one was really expecting to hear, and the only person in the room who didn't turn to the anaesthetist was Rory, too busy concentrating on delivering the baby to turn his head.

'What?' His single word was like a bullet.

'Muscle rigidity, tachycardia…' The anaesthetist was working hard, rapidly pushing drugs into Fiona as he skillfully assessed his patient. Ally felt her heart, which was already racing, go into overdrive as machine alarms started going off. 'We've got an erythematous flush.' The anaesthetist's voice was urgent now as he assessed the reddening of his patient's skin, and Ally could scarcely believe the words she was hearing as he called for more help. 'Get the MH cart!'

Rory was handing Ally the baby now, a boy, just as Fiona had predicted. But his body was flaccid, his colour grey, and Ally rushed him over to the resuscitation cot, trying to block out the sounds going on behind her and look after Fiona's baby as the staff worked on the mother.

MH, or malignant hyperthermia, was a rare and life-threatening emergency that some-times occurred during anaesthetic. The drugs used to anaesthetise the patient triggered a major metabolic crisis and though the cause was unknown—in some cases hereditary—the most worrying thing was that, more often than not, especially if they had never had an anaesthetic before, nothing in the patient's history might indicate that the patient was at risk. And nothing in Fiona's history had even hinted that she might be one of the patients who was susceptible, yet here she lay, her heart rate erratic, her body failing as the anaesthetist replaced the drugs that were known to trigger the event with others, setting up further lines to enable massive lifesaving treatment to be quickly delivered. More backup was being urgently summoned. Eskys of ice were being wheeled in to pack Fiona's body and Ally could scarcely believe she was witnessing this nightmare—that just a few moments ago it had seemed like just another busy morning in Maternity.

So dire was this particular emergency that theatres were stocked with a specific cart containing drugs and necessary equipment, just in case of this rare eventuality, but no one had been expecting to use it—especially today.

'Hyperventilate him.' Hugh was flicking the baby's feet to stimulate him and listening to the baby's chest at the same time as Ally suctioned him and bagged him. Looking down, she could see that even Hugh's usually steady hands were shaking as the theatre staff raced to save Fiona's life—losing a mother was not on anyone's agenda.

'You need to close, Rory.' Another anaesthetist was on hand now, breathless from his mad dash to the obstetric theatre, shouting his orders to Rory who was working on. 'We need her incision closed.'

'She's bleeding out,' Rory shouted back, and Ally caught Hugh's eyes. Rory's finding was ominous. Uncontrollable bleeding was a side effect of MH but in this situation controlling the bleeding was an appalling prospect, with the uterus being so vascular. Packed cells were being put up now, replacing the blood that Fiona was rapidly losing. Clotting agents were being administered, but all of this was occurring in the background. Ally refused to allow herself to dwell on the unfolding drama on the theatre table. She just focused on the tiny life that lay on the resuscitation cot beside her.

Normally, by now Rory would be calling for an update, wanting to know what was happening with the babe, but he was too busy even for that distraction—everyone was. The newborn let out a small fragile cry. It was smothered by the mask Ally was holding over his face and went unheard and unheeded by the rest of the staff as they focused on the child's mother.

'We've got him.' Hugh gave a tiny relieved nod as the infant started to pink up, one glimmer of hope in this otherwise black day. Ally removed the mask and instead held oxygen tubing near the baby's nose and mouth, increasing the oxygen content of the air as he took his first vital unaided breaths. His cries were more lusty now, limbs that had been flaccid were furiously kicking, his little arms jerking at the wide unfamiliar space that surrounded him. As soon as Hugh had completed his examination, Ally weighed and measured him, then wrapped him firmly in a bunny rug. At this point normally she'd have gone outside, would have taken the newborn infant to meet his father, but how on earth could she now?

What on earth could she say to Mark?

So instead she placed the babe in the warmer and quietly observed, offering assistance when she could, running through blood, wheeling a never-ending line of equipment over to the theatre table, and her heart went out to Rory. Sweat was pouring down his brow, his face taut with concentration, huge hands skilful as over and over he tried to close the incision in the uterus and bring the bleeding under control. Finally he gave a small nod, watching for a moment and checking that his sutures were holding in the friable uterus, that blood wasn't filling the abdominal cavity. 'OK, I'm closing.' No neat row of stitches for Fiona. Rory finished the procedure with a rapid line of staples, knowing that Fiona needed this anaesthetic nightmare to be over.

'How's she doing?' His gloves were peeled off and he threw them in the general direction of a stainless-steel bucket, heading over to the top of the theatre table and talking with the anaesthetist. Ally could only guess at his anguish. In a matter of fifteen minutes he seemed to have aged a decade, his eyes hollow in his face, his skin pasty as he listened to what the anaesthetist had to say.

'How's the baby?' Rory looked over at Hugh, who gave him a thumbs-up. 'He had a shaky start, but he's doing fine now. You got him out just in time. I'll take him down to the nursery now and get him out of everyone's way.'

Rory stared around the chaos of the room, the mountain of blood-soaked swabs, empty packets littering every surface, doctors, nurses crowding around his patient, and Fiona somewhere in the middle. Ally watched with tears in her eyes as he went over to the woman and, bending down, said something that was for Fiona's ears only, before standing up and peeling off his mask. He scanned the room for a moment, his eyes finally resting on Ally's as he braced himself to face the hardest part of this awful day.

'Will you come with me while I speak to Mark?'

CHAPTER NINE

THEY walked out of Theatre and into the tiny annexe.

Rory pulled off his blood-soaked theatre gown, but his theatre trousers and top beneath were stained as well, and Ally rummaged through the linen trolley and found him a fresh pair. As Rory quickly changed, not a single word or glance was exchanged between them.

Rory's lips were clamped together as undoubtedly he practised the words in his mind, summoning the strength to deliver a speech that every obstetrician dreaded. Ally stood there, willing herself to be calm, trying to stop the palsied shaking that seemed to be consuming her, knowing she had to be strong here, that it wouldn't be helpful to Mark if she was overly emotional—that was entirely his prerogative.

Down along the polished corridors they walked in silence, and only as they arrived at the interview room door did Rory turn and look at her.

'I don't know if I can do this.'

And she nodded, nodded because she understood, and nodded her encouragement because they both knew that Rory had to.

'Jess says that there's been a complication.' Mark sprang to his feet the second the door opened, and Jess looked over at Rory and Ally, searching their faces for any clues as to what was to come.

'Sit down, Mark.' Rory's voice was firm, guiding the man to his chair and then sitting down opposite him. And even if the speech could have been delivered standing, Ally guessed that it wasn't just for Mark's benefit they were sitting. Her own legs felt as if they were made of jelly so Rory's must be too.

'Jess is right.' He paused for a second and Ally knew he was struggling to compose himself. 'Almost as soon as we started the operation, the anaesthetist noticed some worrying signs in Fiona.'

'Fiona?' Mark's bewildered voice filled the room, terrified eyes darting from Ally to Jess and then back to Rory. 'What about the baby?'

'The baby was delivered quickly,' Rory said gently. 'And the paediatrician was on hand and he's doing OK.'

'So the problem isn't with the baby?' Mark was standing again now, raking his hand through his hair, his breath coming in short rapid bursts as the news started to filter through, as a nightmare he hadn't even contemplated started to descend. 'You're telling me that there are problems with Fiona?'

'Fiona has suffered an extremely rare reaction to anaesthetic, Mark.' Rory's voice was completely even, detached almost as he walked Mark through the minefield of information. 'It's called malignant hyperthermia, or MH. It's when the body reacts to the drugs used in anaesthesia.'

'And is it serious? I mean, can you reverse it?'

Rory stood now, facing Mark head on. 'It's extremely serious, Mark. It causes trouble in many systems in the body—her temperature and blood pressure are elevated and her heart is beating irregularly. We've also had trouble trying to control her bleeding...' Ally knew he was avoiding getting too technical but at the same time attempting to let Mark know the multifaceted problem that the doctors were facing. 'We completed the operation as quickly as we could, but Fiona is very sick indeed. The symptoms progressed extremely rapidly and right now we're struggling to stabilise her.'

'But she'll be OK?' Mark's anguished eyes pleaded with Rory.

'It's way too early to say that,' Rory said gently, holding Mark's eyes when he must have wanted so badly to look away.

'Are you trying to tell me that my wife might die?'

'It's possible, Mark.' Somehow, Rory still looked him in the eye as he nodded. 'We're doing everything we possibly can to save her, but I have to tell you that things don't look good.'

'She came in to have a baby!' Mark was shouting now, his fists clenched in rage and horror, grief literally overwhelming him, and for a flash of time Ally was worried he was going to lose it, that he might even hit Rory. But Rory didn't flinch and Ally guessed that he was also prepared for that eventuality and would stop it before it started. 'My wife trusted you—you never told us this could happen. I'd never have made her sign that form if I thought this was how it was going to turn out!'

'No one expected this to happen,' Rory said, and all the fight seemed to go out of Mark, his body convulsed by sobbing. Rory held onto his shoulders, literally held him up as his whole world fell apart.

'She came in to have a baby,' Mark kept repeating. 'This isn't how it's supposed to be. I don't even know what she had.' Stunned, dazed, he looked from Ally to Rory. 'What did she have?'

Strange that what had once seemed so vitally important was almost immaterial now.

'You had a son,' Rory said softly, lowering Mark back onto his seat. 'And he's beautiful. Would you like Ally to bring him in to you?'

It was a relief to escape for a moment, and when Mark nodded, Ally slipped out and headed over to the nursery, ignoring her colleagues who were all eager for an update, terrified that if she stopped to talk, she'd just break down.

'He wants to see the baby,' Ally said to Vivien, the nurse unit manager, who was actually out of her office and working the floor, most of the staff tied up with emergency. 'Is it OK if I take him down to him?'

'Of course.'

'Have you heard how Fiona is?'

'Not good.' Vivien gave a crisp nod.

'Though they have asked me to organise an air ambulance, which I've just done, so hopefully she's stabilised a touch. I really don't know any more than that and I don't want to get in the way by asking for updates.'

'How's the baby doing?' Ally asked, staring down at the tiny bundle fretting in his cot.

'A bit restless, but his obs are all good.' She was filling in the babe's chart. 'He's actually hungry. Maybe you could ask the dad to sign the consent form so we can give him some formula.'

And even if it was protocol, even if it was hospital policy to obtain a parent's permission before the baby was given formula, Ally could scarcely believe what she was hearing. Vivien might be her senior, but Ally was past caring who she offended right now.

'As if I'm going to ask the dad to sign a petty consent form after what just happened,' Ally snapped, close to tears and angry with everyone. 'Just give him a bottle, Vivien.'

* * *

The interview room was subdued as Ally entered. A theatre nurse was talking to Mark and explaining that the anaesthetists were still working on his wife, but one of them would be along shortly to explain about Fiona's transfer to a major hospital with specialized intensive care facilities.

'That's good, isn't it?' Mark gulped. 'I mean, if she's made it this far.'

'It's a little bit more hopeful,' the nurse said cautiously, 'but there's still an awful long way to go. We're literally taking things minute by minute right now.'

Only then did Mark notice that Ally was in the room. His face slipped as he stared at the small package she was holding in her arms, and Ally wasn't the only one in the room to shed a tear as she handed the babe to his father. Jess's face was purple as she blew into a tissue and Rory sniffed loudly a couple of times as Mark cradled his son for the first time.

'He's beautiful.' Mark stared down at him,

and Ally knelt down beside him, supporting the baby as well, as Mark was shaking so much. 'And he's OK, you said.'

'He's perfect,' Ally agreed. Now was not the time to tell Mark about his son's close call—the baby was fine and for now that was all he needed to know.

'She wanted a son…' Mark's finger traced the tiny snub nose. 'Fiona doesn't even know what she's had. She'd have been so happy to know that she's had a little boy.'

And Ally thought back to the conversation she'd had with Fiona just as she'd been about to be put under, but filed it and saved it for later. She decided to discuss with Jess what to do with that precious piece of information and hoped against hope that Fiona might soon be able to tell Mark herself. She watched as a smile flickered on Mark's face between his tears as his son sucked furiously on his tiny hands. 'Is he hungry?'

'I think so,' Ally said gently. 'Would you like me to bring a bottle so you can feed him?'

she offered, not in the least surprised when Mark shook his head.

'I don't think I can.'

'That's fine—we'll take care of him for now,' Ally said gently, glad she had stood up to Vivien, wondering what Rory's reaction would have been if she'd produced a form now for this poor man to sign.

'Can I go with Fiona—when she's transferred?'

'No, I'm sorry.' Rory shook his head, and answered the difficult question. Sometimes relatives were allowed to travel, even with a desperately ill patient, but not in this case. Fiona's treatment was so intensive there would barely be enough room for the equipment and staff. 'She'll be going by helicopter—there will be a lot of staff and a lot of activity on board.'

'Do you want me to ring someone for you?' Jess offered. 'You shouldn't be facing this on you own, Mark. One of your relatives could drive you into the city.'

'Our families are both in Sydney.' Mark shook his head.

'What about a friend?'

Again Mark shook his head, staring down at his son as he spoke. 'I don't really want to tell anyone just yet but I don't think I can drive. I'll call a taxi…'

'I'll take you,' Rory cut in. 'I'll go and arrange cover and I'll take you there myself.'

As he walked out of the interview room Ally caught Jess's worried look.

'*Go,*' she mouthed, telling Ally to go after him, then, talking so that everyone could hear, she added, 'I'll stay here with Mark and the baby.'

'Rory!' Ally had to run to catch up with him. 'I know you want to help, but you're needed here. We've got other women labouring, the ward's fit to burst, we need patients to be discharged…'

'Then Mr Davies can come in from the golf course and do it!' Rory snapped back, staring somewhere over her shoulder, refusing to meet her eyes.

'You can't just step down. You're an obstetrician, Rory, not a taxi driver. I know you feel awful for Mark, we all do—'

'I can't do this.' Rory slapped his hands on his thighs and turned to go.

'It's your job,' Ally pointed out.

'Well, maybe I don't want it any more— maybe I don't want to be a registrar.'

'Rory, you're not making sense.'

'Just leave it, Ally.'

'You can't just walk off!'

'Watch me.' Rory's face was chalk white, a muscle pounding in his cheek as he still refused to look at her. 'I'm not cut out for this, for any of this, Ally.' Some sixth sense told her that he wasn't just talking about work. 'It's just not me.'

'We'll talk about it tonight, Rory. We can discuss it at home when things have calmed down,' Ally said, but as Rory shook his head Ally knew what was coming next, knew because when finally he forced himself to look at her it was as if a glass wall had been placed between them, because even though he was just a few inches away, the distance was huge. She knew as he shook his head what was coming next, and she braced herself for his second cruel rejection.

'I'm not cut out for *any* of this, Ally.'

'Does that include me?' He gave a slow nod and somehow she stayed standing as again he broke her heart. 'Work, relationships…it's just not me. I can't see myself in five years as a consultant…'

'You don't have to be one if you don't want to—' Ally said, but he broke her off with the cruellest line of them all, 'And I can't see myself with you either, Ally.'

CHAPTER TEN

THE rest of the day seemed interminable and Ally had to drag on every last piece of her reserves to perform one of the hardest tasks in nursing—comforting patients when you needed it yourself, smiling, carrying on, reassuring them over and over when your own heart was bleeding.

'I heard a patient was sick and I saw Mark in tears in the corridor.' Kathy was as frantic as she was inconsolable, her looming depression and friendship with Fiona making the unpalatable news worse, if that was at all possible. 'It's Fiona, isn't it?'

Ally sat down on the edge of the bed and nodded. Word had spread like wildfire, the patients had all heard the frantic overhead chimes, seen the staff running towards Theatre, witnessed the helicopter landing. To deny it would be futile.

'Fiona became unwell in Theatre—she's been transferred to one of the bigger hospitals in the city and Mark's gone to be with her.'

'And the baby?'

'He's doing well,' Ally said, glad to be able to give one piece of good news at least. 'He's here in the nursery.'

'Why hasn't he gone with Fiona?' Kathy said. 'She'll be devastated to leave him behind. Does she even know?'

'Fiona's not well enough to look after him right now and the baby will be better off here in the nursery than on a ward with other sick people.' Deliberately Ally dodged the latter question, also avoiding the words 'intensive care'. She certainly had no desire to volunteer information. 'So we'll keep the baby here for now and hopefully Fiona will be back soon to look after him herself.'

'But what happened?' Kathy pushed. 'What

went wrong? Why did she have to have a Caesarean section?'

'Kathy, I can't discuss it with you—the same way I wouldn't discuss your care with another patient. All I can tell you is that Fiona is receiving the best treatment possible.'

'Poor Fiona,' Kathy sobbed. 'And poor Mark. God, I've been such an idiot, sitting here moaning when I should have realised at the time just how lucky I was.'

'Don't even think about that,' Ally soothed. 'That's not going to help anyone, is it? Right now you need to concentrate on you and your lovely baby. I see that Rinska's taken you off the antibiotics. You'll be able to feed him in a couple of days once they're all out of your system.'

'I'm going home tomorrow,' Kathy gulped. 'Rinska rang a lactation consultant and she's going to come to my house if I'm having trouble getting him to take the breast.'

'I'm sure you'll be fine.' Ally gave an encouraging smile. 'It might be a bit tricky at first, but young Toby's got a very experienced mum.' Her diversion tactics only worked for a couple of moments. Kathy's questions about Fiona started again and in the end Ally was grateful when Jess poked her head around the door and reminded Ally that her shift should have ended half an hour ago.

There was just one job to do before Ally left the ward—fill in the admission book. Ally looked at her own casual writing of that morning, listing Fiona's name and the date of admission in smart black pen. Clicking her pen to red to show there had been a serious event, Ally filled in the rest of details with a heavy heart.

Live male.

Mother transferred to Royal Women's Hospital.

'Have we heard any more news from the Women's Hospital?' Ally asked, joining an equally weary Jess at the lockers.

'"Critical".' Jess tutted. 'That's all they'll say when we ring—as if we didn't know that much already. I hate the way the nurses on

Intensive Care just take over, and forget we were the ones looking after her. Well, they'd better have a bit more information soon. I've already warned the girls on the late shift that we'll be ringing later this evening for news. I'm not going to be able to make it all night without knowing.'

'Me neither,' Ally sighed, hoping that by the time she got home Rory would be there and could bring her up to speed.

Hoping that by the time she got home Rory would have calmed down. She was literally shaking inside. As she walked to the lift Ally felt as if she was climbing off the biggest roller-coaster ride of her life, scarcely able to believe that the shift that had started so beautifully had ended so tragically. And she couldn't even begin to deal with Rory's little bombshell about the two of them. Her mind was completely scrambled, her head spinning as she walked away from the ward.

'I've been a midwife for twenty years and

I've never had a mother die.' Tears were sparkling in Jess's eyes as she pushed the button for the lift. 'I've had some become sick, of course, but normally there's been some warning, a heart condition or something, but for a perfectly healthy woman to come in to give birth and just…'

'She isn't dead,' Ally said firmly, but her heart wasn't really in it. Over and over images of Fiona's pale, mottled body on the theatre table as bag after bag of blood and fluid had been pushed into her played in Ally's mind, and not for the first time she wondered if the only person she was fooling with her forced optimism was herself.

Seeing Rory's hire car badly parked in her driveway, Ally let herself in the door, not knowing what to expect when she saw him, and devastated to see his bags packed and lined up in the hallway. However, it was nothing she hadn't been expecting.

'Leaving again?' She managed a twist of sarcasm as Rory met her in the hallway. 'Well,

I can't say it's come as a complete surprise. After all, I've had enough practice.'

'Don't,' Rory attempted. 'Ally, it's not you, it's me.'

'I know it's not me with the problem, Rory,' Ally flared. 'I'm just the idiot who trusted you all over again. When did you decide it was a mistake, Rory?' She watched his face stiffen. 'Or didn't you even care what it might do to me, just so long as you were satisfied?' Anger rose in her, and even though she'd sworn she wouldn't do this, Ally let him have it—just a little bit—let him glimpse some of the hell he was putting her through. 'I believed every word you told me!' Ally shouted. 'I let you twist everything around until in the end I doubted even myself—really thought that perhaps I'd misjudged you all those years ago. But it turns out that the only person I misjudged was myself, because I was sure I'd never let you hurt me again.'

'I never intended to hurt you,' Rory tried, but

Ally just laughed, a spiteful, mirthless laugh that didn't suit her.

'I believe you, Rory. In fact, I think you're so used to doing it that you don't even have to try.'

'I thought I could do it. I came back because I really thought I was ready to make a commitment—'

'I don't want to hear it, Rory.' Ally shook her head. 'I really don't want to stand here and listen as you attempt to justify what you just did to me.'

'You're the one who said this morning that you shouldn't judge until you're armed with the facts.'

'Thanks for reminding me,' Ally snapped. 'Thanks for reminding me that I was already angry with you before Fiona was taken ill.' She swallowed the bile that seemed to be choking her. 'Where are you going—the doctors' mess?'

Rory shook his head. 'I'm going to stay in some serviced apartments—I need to get my head around a few things.'

'How's Fiona?' Ally asked, because, despite all that was happening in her life, today Fiona mattered more. 'And, please, don't tell me "critical". I can find that much out by myself.'

'That's about all I know—she's on a ventilator, they're trying to control her temperature and bring her blood pressure down. Apparently she could even have another crisis.'

'God!' Ally ran a weary hand through her hair, her own problems not exactly fading into insignificance but for now at least taking a back seat. 'This shouldn't have happened.'

'I know.' Rory's lips barely moved as he spoke. 'Maybe you were right. Maybe I should have tried the external version, given Fiona a chance for a normal delivery.'

'Rory?' Ally shook her head as if to clear it, frowning at the self-doubt in his usually confident voice. 'I never suggested an external version to Fiona—she's the one I was telling you about who was panicking in antenatal class—that's when I mentioned it. I didn't say anything this morning to her, because I knew it wasn't possible. The baby had to be born, you had no choice but to operate.' Two vertical lines were deepening on the bridge of her nose as realisation started to strike. 'Rory, when I said that it should never have happened, I meant in the greater scheme of things. In no way was I blaming you—surely you know that this wasn't your fault! Maternal death is everyone's worst nightmare. Of course you're feeling awful, but you *cannot* blame yourself.'

'When the coroner might do it for me?'

'You did nothing wrong,' Ally said. 'You know that.'

'All I know is that I can't do it.' Rory stared back at her and despite his bulk he looked as lost and helpless as a little boy. 'I can't go back there, Ally.' And it dawned on her then that he wasn't just walking out on her but on his job, on his life—Rory was walking away from everything. 'I'll ring Mr Davies and tell him tomorrow.'

'Ring him?' Ally checked.

'I don't want to set foot in the place again.'

'Rory, you're overreacting,' Ally attempted, but it only seemed to enrage him.

'A woman's lying at death's door, that little baby probably isn't going to have a mother, so don't try and tell me that I'm overreacting. Ally, I came into obstetrics to prevent this type of thing, to ensure that...' He swallowed whatever it was he'd been about to say and rammed the palms of his hands against his temples. 'I've got to go.'

Ally knew there was no point trying to reason with him, knew that in this mood he wasn't going to listen. And even if he was breaking her heart all over again, it didn't mean she could suddenly stop caring, so as he picked up his bags and made to leave Ally halted him.

'Will you do one thing for me?' If he hadn't been walking out on her for the second time, if he hadn't deep down known how appallingly he was treating her, Ally was sure that Rory wouldn't have even listened to her request. But instead he put down his bags and listened as Ally picked up the phone and offered it to him. 'Can you ring Mr Davies and tell him that you're sick—that you won't be able to come in tomorrow?'

'Another day isn't going to change things, Ally. I know how I feel.'

'Then it's no big deal to do as I ask, is it?' Ally said. 'Surely you can do that much for me at least?'

But he couldn't even give her that. Ignoring the phone she was holding out and picking up his bags, he headed for the door.

'I'll think about it.'

Maybe your brain decided when it had had enough, Ally decided, waking the next morning after an amazingly good sleep and stepping into the shower. Maybe your brain knew when it was completely overloaded and just switched off.

She'd rung the hospital around eight p.m. only to be greeted with the same 'critical' line, but thankfully the word 'stable' had been added. Ally tried not to read too much into it, but it was the most encouraging thing she'd heard since things had gone so drastically wrong for Fiona. Lying on top of her bed, hoping to close her eyes for five minutes to get rid of the most appalling headache, Ally had woken up some nine hours later—an hour before her alarm would have gone off, had she thought to set it. Unable to get back to sleep, she decided to use the precious hour for a slow walk along the beach.

And it helped, just as it always had, just as it always would.

Watching the sun come up, just as it always did.

She'd miss Rory for ever. Picking up a handful of stones and tossing them into the water, Ally knew that for once she wasn't being over-dramatic. She'd miss him for ever because she loved him.

But she loved herself more.

Loved herself too much to put herself through it again, to spend endless days and nights in angst over what had gone wrong, trying to decipher what she could have done differently to make him want to stay.

Rory hadn't wanted to stay and that was reason enough to let him go without a fuss.

She wished Sheba was there, as she watched a dog bounding along the shoreline, wagging his tail, a massive stick in his smiling mouth. How she wished she had her friend by her side just long enough to see her through this next bit of her life.

CHAPTER ELEVEN

THE ward was a bit subdued but running pretty normally. The patients were a touch quieter, asking how Fiona was, the staff gathering for a brief update on her progress. But on the whole it was business as usual, hospital being the one place where in the face of tragedy it was used to carrying on.

'Where's Rory?' Rinska asked, looking crisp in her white coat, waiting for morning rounds to start, and Ally looked up as Vivien answered.

'He called in sick this morning and spoke to Mr Davies. Apparently he's got some gastro bug—hopefully he'll stay away till it's completely cleared. Gastro sweeping the ward is the last thing I need. Right.' Vivien nodded as

Mr Davies arrived. 'Let's get the ward round out of the way.'

Ally was more than happy to be out of the delivery ward today. Maybe Vivien did have a heart, Ally decided, because she'd put her in the nursery where the pace was pretty gentle. She supervised the mums while they bathed their infants, a couple of babies were under phototherapy lights to correct their jaundice and, of course, there was baby Anderson to feed and cuddle.

'How's his mum?' Win finally asked after she'd cleaned around his cot for what must have been the fiftieth time, waiting till the place was quiet so she could talk with Ally, who was feeding one of the sleepy jaundiced infants.

'Still no more news.' Ally gave an apologetic smile as the old lady's face fell. 'Mr Davies is going to ring after lunch and speak to the consultant and hopefully we'll know a bit more then.'

'Has his dad been in?'

'No.' Ally didn't really want to discuss it, but she knew Win's concern was genuine. 'He's staying at his wife's bedside for now—he's rung a few times to see how his son is, though.'

'Poor man,' Win sighed, gazing at the babe as she practically dug a hole in the floor around his crib with her mop.

'Win.' Ally tutted at her own thoughtlessness. 'With all that happened yesterday, I completely forgot to ask. How did your meeting go with your supervisor?'

'Really well.' The old lady beamed. 'I didn't want to say anything yesterday, it seemed wrong somehow to be singing about my good news with this poor little pet's mum so sick, but they're letting me drop my hours.'

'Really?' A smile broke out on her face, but then she frowned, worried for Win that she'd somehow misunderstood, because when Ally had last spoken with Vivien, the result had been a forgone conclusion. 'You mean here, not down in Emergency.'

'Here!' Win was still beaming. 'One day a

week, either a Saturday or Sunday. They even said that they were sorry for all the worry they've caused me.'

'Good for you!' Ally said.

'They didn't mean a word of it.' Win laughed. 'But at least they said it and I know who I've got to thank for it—I've been looking for him all morning. Where's Dr Rory?'

'He's off sick,' Ally answered.

'Sick!' Win tutted. 'Not Dr Rory—he's as strong as an ox.'

'He's got a touch of gastro,' Ally said quickly, torn between revealing too much and keeping Win quiet. Anyway, it wasn't as if she was breaking a confidence, Ally consoled herself. Rory didn't have gastro and, Ally realised as the domestic carried on talking, Win thought the same.

'He's upset about yesterday! He's got himself all worked up about Mrs Anderson.'

'He hasn't,' Ally snapped, wishing Win would just put a lid on it. 'He's got nothing to feel guilty about.'

'I never *said* he felt guilty,' Win huffed. 'Just that he was upset. It would have really affected him.'

'It's affected us all,' Ally said, attempting to drag the conversation back to safer territory 'Anyway, what has Rory got to do with you being able to change your hours?'

'He told them a few home truths!' Win checked they had the place to themselves before speaking in a dramatic whisper. 'My friend was cleaning in the next room…'

'With a glass to the wall.' Ally grinned.

'Probably, knowing Ethel! Anyway, Rory apparently told them that he'd just stopped the hospital appearing on this evening's news show and if they didn't sort out my contract, he'd be going on the show himself to tell them how badly they were treating me…'

'He said that!'

'And more.' Win's smile almost split her face. 'Anyway, the bottom line is that I'm staying right here on Maternity and I've got the hours I wanted. I'm so lucky.'

'No, Win, we're lucky to have you.' And Ally was speaking the truth—as annoying and immovable as Win could be at times, she was a part of this ward and could be leant on in difficult times. Only yesterday, when the ward had been in chaos, Win had taken it on herself to do an extra tea round, chatting and reassuring anxious mums. She'd even answered a couple of call bells, and when it was all over had made sure that every doctor and nurse involved in the drama had had a cup of coffee in front of them as one by one they'd collapsed in the maternity staffroom.

No job description that Admin drew up could define what she did.

'He's fretting for his mum, Ally,' Win said, as baby Anderson started to cry.

'He's just hungry, Win,' Ally answered. 'I'll just finish off this little guy and then I'll be with him.'

'OK.' Win peered into the cot. 'Is there anything I can do for you, Ally?'

'I'm fine, Win,' Ally answered. 'I'll just take

this one in to Mum for a quick cuddle before I put him back under the lights.'

Which was easier said than done. The baby's mother was just coming out of the bath, and naturally Ally waited as she dressed, chatting to her about her son's progress, and on the way back to the nursery was waylaid by Rinska who needed her to hold a nervous patient's hand as she put in an IV. Wishing Rinska would speed things along, Ally glanced anxiously at the clock, relieved when finally the IV was taped in and she could race down the corridor. As she did, Ally was half expecting to hear the infant wailing from the nurses' station. Normally babies' tears didn't faze her, they were part and parcel of working on a maternity ward, but everyone on the ward felt an added responsibility towards Fiona's baby, and the last thing Ally wanted was to leave him crying—for his mother's sake.

The only sound to greet her was one of contented silence. Win had her back to her, sitting in one of the nursing chairs and rocking the baby boy, gazing out at the ocean view and talking happily to him. Maybe it wasn't *appropriate* for a domestic to be nursing a baby, but neither was it *appropriate* for a newborn's mother to be lying critically ill in Intensive Care, and Win had put on a clean nurse's gown and Ally was completely confident that she'd washed her hands.

'I'm sorry I was so long.' Ally slipped in quietly, gesturing for Win to relax as she shot Ally a guilty anxious look.

'I washed my hands and put on a gown,' Win flustered. 'He was crying his eyes out and I thought what I'd want me to do if I was his mother…'

'It's fine, Win,' Ally said, knowing that Win wasn't going to make a habit of it. 'It would be great if you could hold him for me while I warm his bottle.'

'I'd like that,' Win said. 'Poor little duck.'

'She might be OK,' Ally ventured.

'I hope to God she is,' Win replied. 'In all the years I've been here, I've only ever see it

254 THE MIDWIFE'S SPECIAL DELIVERY

happen once, and I prayed that I'd never see it again. Thirty-one years ago it happened, almost to the very day…

'You always remember those sorts of dates,' Win carried on as Ally checked the bottle on her wrist. 'The same way you remember your kids' birthdays.'

'Thanks.' Ally took the babe from Win, and settled herself in a seat, popping a cloth nappy under his chin and giving the hungry babe what he wanted.

'Not just your kids, mind,' Win added, taking off her gown and pushing her mop and bucket out of the nursery. 'It could be anyone you care about.'

'Sorry?' Ally frowned up at Win, not sure that what she was supposed to have missed here.

'I was just saying that you always remember certain dates—February the twenty-seventh—will stay in my mind for ever.'

It would stay in her mind too, but for different reasons entirely, Ally thought as Win finally shuffled off. February the twenty-seventh was Rory's birthday—Win was right—it was one of those dates you always remembered. Rory the Pisces, another star sign she automatically checked.

'Need a hand?' Jess was at the door. 'It's pretty quiet out there.'

Ally was about to wave her away, to tell her there was nothing that needed to be done, but like tiny hailstones on a tin roof tiny snippets of information were raining in her mind, impossibility drenching her as she struggled to shrug it all off—to convince herself that, not for the first time in her life, where Rory was concerned, she was overreacting.

'Can you feed Baby Anderson for me?' Clearly upset, she appealed to Jess, who took the babe without question. 'There's something I need to know.'

Win was nowhere in sight and, glancing at her watch, Ally guessed she was down in the canteen right now, enjoying her coffee-break and sharing her good news with her colleagues. Ally was just about to head down there, to find Win and ask her to tell her what she knew, but as she passed the storeroom Ally knew that she didn't need to, knew she could find out the truth as she would prefer to—in private.

She'd organised the admission records carefully—each book filed according to date—and it only took a couple of moments to locate the book in question. Balancing on the ladder, Ally hauled it down, but her hand was shaking so much it took for ever to turn the dusty old pages, looking at the neat inscriptions, row after row of names written in navy or black.

Except one.

Staring at the neat red writing, the words seemed to blur before her and Ally rummaged in her pocket for a tissue, wiping her eyes and blowing her nose and bracing herself to face the truth.

Lola Donovan, age 25
Admitted Feb 27th

Deceased Feb 27th
Live male infant

Beside her name, a nurse or doctor, or whoever the initials A.S. belonged to, had written 'RIP' and Ally knew, because of yesterday, the pain that was etched within them, how much the staff that had nursed Lola that day would have been touched for the rest of their lives by the tragic outcome when they had unwittingly signed up for that shift. And if Rory's reaction hadn't made sense before, it made a little bit now—losing a mother was what every one of the obstetric team dreaded most, but for Rory it must have been hell.

And, yes, she felt sorry for him, yes, it was appalling, but as she sat there, staring at the neat writing and reading a little bit of Rory's history, unexpectedly Ally felt anger—anger that he had placed himself in such a vulnerable position, almost set himself up for this possible fall, given himself an opportunity to walk away...

Closing the book, feeling like an intruder,

Ally put it back in its place and stared at the neat row of books that were mainly filled with joy, but occasionally marred by a pain that touched everyone.

For ever.

Stumbling out into the corridor, her face ashen in the fluorescent light, Vivien's concerned face was the one that greeted her first.

'Jess said that you seemed upset. I've been trying to find you to tell you that we've heard from the Women's Hospital. Fiona Anderson is still very sick but the word is she's going to pull through.' It was the news Ally had scarcely dared hope for. She'd never seen someone as close to death as Fiona actually live, had never in her career seen someone beat such appalling odds and come through, but, then again, Fiona had a lot to live for. 'I thought you might like to be the one to let the baby know!'

And whether he understood or not, Ally told him, held the little boy close and told him that his mum was doing well and that just as soon as she could she'd come back to him. Tears streaming down her face, Ally wished she could share the good news with the other person who really needed to hear it. Only it wasn't her place to tell him anything any more.

Rory had made that choice when he'd walked out on her for the second time.

CHAPTER TWELVE

ALLY didn't want to be at work—her maudlin mood not quite fitting for Maternity—but she did her absolute best, smiling and chatting with a new admission, checking the expectant mother's obs and going through her birthing plan, trying hard to portray all the confidence she'd had only yesterday, to have as much faith in Mother Nature as she had before and be as positive of a good outcome as she had been before it had all gone so tragically wrong for Fiona.

It was a relief when her shift ended.

A relief to pull off her name tag and step out into the late afternoon sun, a relief to finally be able to stop smiling.

But as much as she'd willed her shift to end,

Ally didn't particularly want to go home either, didn't want to face the silence of an empty house with no Sheba staggering down the hall to greet her, no Rory to moan at about the mess he'd left in the kitchen, just a pile of jumbled thoughts that Ally didn't have the mental energy to examine.

Instead of going home, Ally drove to the shopping centre. She toyed with the idea of ringing Becky and Donna to meet for coffee, while knowing she couldn't—the information Win had directed her to, the news she had supposedly stumbled upon, not really hers to share.

When even fifteen minutes of trying on shoes in her favourite store failed to cheer her up, Ally gave in, buying instead the biggest bar of chocolate she could find and giving herself a good talking-to as she walked along.

One more night to wallow in self-pity, Ally decided.

One more night of feeling sorry for herself and that would be it!

She'd already wasted three years on Rory and she certainly wasn't about to go there again—Rory Donovan didn't deserve it.

Her glimmer of optimism lasted all the way to the pet shop. Staring in the window, a ghost of a smile played on her lips as she watched three tiny puppies nuzzling together, each one vying for the warmest spot—each one missing its mother.

God, why did everything have to make her cry?

Why wasn't she standing here and thinking about baby Anderson or Sheba now?

Why did every road lead to Rory?

The house, as Ally predicted, was gloomily quiet, no tail thumping on the wicker basket, not even that appalling, musty, old-dog smell to chase away by opening windows and lighting some incense. Placing her chocolate in the fridge, Ally showered and changed into shorts and a T-shirt, and after pulling on a pair of flat sandals she filled a water bottle and headed for the beach, for the first time in living memory not even bothering with mascara, hoping a brisk walk and another good talking-to might clear her head a bit. She only made it a few steps, remembering in an instant the last time she'd been here with poor old Sheba, who had tried bravely to pretend she had been enjoying herself for the sake of her mistress. Ally gave up trying to be brave. Sitting down on the sand, she pushed Rory and Fiona and baby Anderson aside and cried for her old friend, the one soul she'd always confided in. The one soul who really understood.

'Ally?' Rory's tentative voice was neither expected nor welcome, and she pointedly didn't look up, just sniffed loudly, squinting into the low sun as Rory sat down on the beach beside her.

'I'm not crying about you,' she said finally, still refusing to look at him. 'In case that's what you think. I'm crying about Sheba.'

'I know.'

'After yesterday and everything, I never really got the chance to mourn her.'

'You don't have to explain your tears to me,' Rory said, and Ally nodded.

'You're right—I don't.'

She wouldn't have looked at him—in fact, Ally was determined not to look at him. Pride, coupled with naked eyelashes, was enough incentive to stare fixedly ahead. But the sound of whimpering noises coming from Rory's direction got the better of her and, turning around briefly, Ally stared at a pink nose jutting out of a box Rory was attempting to keep closed on his knee.

'I don't want a puppy, Rory,' Ally snapped. 'If I want another dog then I'll go out and buy one for myself when I'm good and ready.'

'It might not be for you,' Rory said, pushing the lid down on the box. 'I might have got it for me.'

'I doubt it,' Ally bristled. 'Dogs take commitment, Rory, which is something you appear a little short of! You can't just up and go when you feel like it when you've got a dog. You can't just decide you want to hop on a plane or stay out for a couple of nights just because you feel like it.' Her voice was rising a bit now. 'You can't just walk away because all of a sudden you've changed your mind!'

'I'm aware of that,' Rory said, trying to catch her eye, but Ally wouldn't even give him that, ignoring the puppy's whimpers and jerking her head back towards the bay. 'But I've decided that I'm ready for that sort of commitment now. Mr Davies rang to ask when I'd be back and I told him tomorrow.'

'He told you the good news about Fiona?'

'He did,' Rory said. 'But even before I'd heard that, I'd made up my mind that I was coming back to work. I completely over-reacted yesterday. I came to say thank you to you for preventing me making a big mistake—I could have really messed up my job.'

'That's what you came here to say?' Ally asked, the stupid jolt of hope that had unwittingly flared when he'd joined her on the beach seeping out of her like a leaky balloon—as if Rory was going to come bearing gifts, as if Rory Donovan was about to apologize to a woman for breaking her heart.

Again!

'That, and sorry.' It was Rory avoiding looking at her now. 'For walking out on you.'

'Which time?' Ally asked ungraciously.

'Both times,' Rory answered. 'Ally, I haven't been completely open with you.'

'You haven't been at all open with me,' Ally corrected, and Rory's breath whistled through his clenched teeth.

'You're not making this very easy, Ally.'

'Why should I make it easy?' Hurt eyes met his. 'Why should I make this easy for you when it's been hell for me?'

'I said those things because I was upset yesterday. I know we were all upset, but it hit me especially hard.' Rory took a deep breath and Ally held hers, knowing what was coming next and willing herself to hold it together, to not give in to the tears that were threatening. 'My mother died during childbirth, Ally.'

She didn't say that she already knew, didn't say anything at all for a moment, just bit hard on her lip as Rory tentatively continued.

'She had a heart attack during labour. Apparently she had undiagnosed mitral stenosis. It didn't show up until the post-mortem.'

'I'm sorry,' Ally gulped, and it would have been the easiest thing to fall into his arms, to cry with him for all he had lost and all he had been through, but the path of least resistance wasn't what was needed here. If they were ever to get ahead, they had to face the obstacles square on, stand up to the enemy and defeat it.

'Ally, do you understand now why—?'

'No.' She stopped him right there, had to say what she had to say and now was the time to do it. 'No, I don't understand.'

'You're not even trying to,' Rory pointed out, but Ally wasn't about to be deflected that easily.

'What do you want, Rory? For me to say, "Oh, that explains it, then" or, "That makes it OK"? Well, it doesn't make it OK. If anything, it makes it worse.'

'Worse?' Rory frowned back at her.

'Worse.' Ally nodded. 'Yes, there was a reason for you to be upset yesterday, yes, there was a reason for you to lose it and threaten to give up your job, but the fact of the matter is you never shared that reason with me. In all the years we've known each other you've held back what's probably the biggest piece of you, leaving me to join up the numbers.'

'I know.' Rory stood up. 'I thought if I came here and explained, maybe you'd understand, maybe we could scrap what I said yesterday and start again.'

Mascara or no mascara, Ally blinked up at him. 'Till the next time?'

'What next time?' Rory frowned.

'The next time something goes wrong in your life, the next time something happens and you decide to walk instead of talk. If yesterday was an isolated incident, then maybe I could accept it, Rory, but it was just a repeat of what happened three years ago. What was your excuse then, Rory?'

'I've already told you.'

His back was to the low sun and Ally had to put up her hand to shield her eyes, his face unreadable in the shadow.

'When?' Ally snapped.

'Just then.'

She frowned up at him, trying to recall the conversation, shaking her head at what must have been so fleeting it had been missed.

'I don't ever want to have a baby.' Rory's voice was unwavering. 'I'm positive about that.'

'That's your prerogative, Rory,' Ally said. 'But what on earth has that got to do with what happened three years ago?'

'Because I felt the same then as I do now. Look at you, Ally, you're barely five foot two and look at me.'

'Sorry?'

'You're tiny. If you had my child…'

'Rory.' Blinking in the harsh sunlight, Ally frowned back at him. 'I wanted an honest relationship with you and we barely made it through the first night. I wasn't thinking about what type of babies we'd be making.'

'I was.'

The directness of his statement shook her to the very core—forced Ally to examine her own honesty in all of this, because she *had* been thinking about the type of babies they'd make—oh, not all of the time, hardly at all really, but every now and then she'd let her imagination wander to that delicious, elusive place and picture herself pregnant by Rory.

'Rory, I…' The words strangled in her throat, her strong, brave stance crumbling as the truth was realised, as finally he revealed to her his biggest fear. Sitting down again beside her, he took a moment before going on, a moment both of them needed, because Ally's mind seemed to have frozen, her mind stalling as she tried to fathom what he was telling her.

'It was always relatively easy to walk away from a relationship. As soon as marriage or babies were even hinted at, it was my cue to end it. Sometimes I even managed to convince myself that a life-long relationship wasn't what I wanted…'

'Sometimes?'

'Whenever I wasn't thinking about you.' Tears were swimming in his eyes as he held her gaze. 'Mother Earth with attitude!' He gave a regretful smile. 'Ally, within a few months of moving in with you I knew how easy it would be to get serious about you. I broke up with Gloria because I'd met someone else that I like—you.'

'You broke up with Gloria because of me?'

'Because of you.' Rory nodded.

'And you didn't think to tell me?' She was angry all over again, angry at him for holding back on her, angry at the years he'd wasted. 'You're telling me that you decided we weren't going to have a future together because my pelvis wasn't wide enough for you, because of my lack of childbearing hips…' She stopped talking as Rory laughed, a tear-filled laugh but a laugh just the same, and Ally managed a weak smile, too.

'It's a bit more complicated than that but, yep, that about sums it up.'

'I could always have a Caesarean.' It was an attempt at a feeble joke but after what had happened yesterday it all came out wrong. And the sort of laugh he'd managed died then, and so did Ally's smile.

'I couldn't take that chance with you, Ally, couldn't bear if what happened to my mother…'

'It wasn't your fault,' Ally whispered, and Rory nodded.

'I know that,' Rory said. 'I know that! The sensible, medical part of me knows that, but at the end of the day…' His hand gripped hers. 'I wasn't exactly small. I heard my dad talking to my grandmother once, saying that…'

And despite her vow that she wouldn't cry in front of him about it, despite the anger for all the years he'd made them waste, Ally cried then, cried for his pain, cried for a little boy who had grown up with guilt etched on his heart, without a mum to tell him that it was never, nor could it ever have been, his fault.

'Rory, it happened. And like the same way it happened to Fiona, no one could have predicted it and no one could have prevented it. I've spent years working in midwifery, safe in my little cocoon, utterly convinced that there was way too much intervention, that birthing was a completely natural process that women had been doing since the beginning of time...' Ally gulped as the firm rules she'd practised her craft by blurred a little. 'Women have been dying since the beginning of time, too—and even though, with modern medicine, with proper antenatal care and monitoring, yes, the risks are minuscule, there are still no written guarantees. I see that now. But you knew the risks all along, you've lived your life knowing them. I just don't understand why you went into obstetrics, knowing what you know, knowing how devastated you'd be if it happened.'

'Because I thought I could somehow prevent it.' Rory swallowed. 'You're right, though. When I first went into medicine, obstetrics was the last field I thought I'd be specialising in, but when I did my rotation I found out I really loved it, and I guess a part of me thought that in some way I could make a difference somehow…'

'Honour your mum?' Ally suggested softly.

'Sounds like a bit of an ego trip, doesn't it?'

'I don't think so.' Ally smiled. 'I've seen you work, remember. I know how much you care about your patients. Yes, we may clash every now and then and, yes, I might think you're a bit heavy-handed with the monitors and pain control, but I can truthfully say that if I was in labour, you're the doctor I'd want to see.'

'You won't be in labour, though.' Rory visibly winced. 'I couldn't bear it, Ally. Couldn't live for nine months dreading the outcome. You want babies, your own babies, you know that you do…'

'Rory, I want you.' Ally's voice was unwavering. 'I've always wanted you, baby or no baby. If you don't want children, I can accept that.'

'But can you?' Rory shook his head. 'It's easy to say that now, but in a few years you might change your mind.'

'I might,' Ally said, looking at this big proud man who was so scared inside, and finally, after the longest time, she understood where he was coming from. 'And then I'll remind myself how I felt today, how I felt for the three years you were gone, and then I'll know that, baby or no baby, I made the right choice. Anyway…' Ally sniffed, tears streaming down her face, but she forced a smile. 'We could keep dogs! We could be one of those strange couples who put bows in their dogs' hair and dress them in little coats, tell all our friends how clever they are…'

'It wouldn't be enough.'

'Who knows?' Ally smiled out at the ocean. 'The only thing I do know is I'm not waiting another three years for you to make up your mind, Rory. If you turn your back on us again, then so will I. I've spent the last three years waiting for your call and I have no intention of hitting thirty and finding myself still staring at the phone. Here we are sitting talking about babies and we haven't even managed to sleep in the same bed two nights in a row.'

'Are you propositioning me?' Rory grinned and it was the nicest smile she'd ever seen, a flash of the old Rory who could always at a thousand paces melt her heart. 'Because, if you are…' His voice trailed off, and Ally realised that she'd lost her audience now. The puppy, thoroughly fed up with his box, was yapping loudly, and Rory was lifting the lid and peering inside.

'It's for me really, isn't it?' Ally asked hopefully, but her expectant smile turned to one of horror as Rory lifted the lid and pulled the tiny grey and white pup out. Ally stared at the pink beady eyes that matched the snuffling nose, curls already coiling in its coat, and the biggest paws she'd ever seen on a dog.

'Rory, have you any idea what you've bought?'

'A dog.' Rory grinned again, putting the little guy down and hovering over him like a proud parent as he bounded around in the sand, squatting and yapping at Ally, pink eyes pleading for her to love him.

'It's an old English sheepdog, Rory,' Ally gasped. 'It's going to weigh a ton. It will eat you out of house and home…'

'I can't actually keep pets at the apartments.' Rory gave an apologetic grimace 'You're right—I *did* buy it for you.'

'Rory, this dog's going to be huge!' Ally exclaimed, pushing him away as Rory held him up to her face. 'No, I don't want to hold him, because if I do I'll get attached and then I won't be able to let him go. Just get rid of him, Rory!'

'The guy at the store said that, despite their

size, they're very affectionate,' Rory said, and the double meaning wasn't lost on Ally. 'They're devoted, in fact, and, according to the shopkeeper, once they accept who's the boss they're apparently very easy to train. He did say that they get lonely, though—they love to have a mate. We could have two—they could have matching bows!'

'We?' Ally checked.

'We.' Rory nodded. 'If you're sure you want him.'

'I do want him,' Ally sobbed, and she didn't need to be strong any more because Rory was holding her, the puppy squirming between them as Rory kissed her hair, her eyes, her lips, and together they made up their minds, in unison they said the words that both wanted to hear…

'Let's take him home.'

EPILOGUE

'YOU told me it wouldn't hurt!' Coming out of the lift, Ally leant against the wall and groaned as another pain hit. 'You told me that I'd be having a planned Caesarean, you promised that I wouldn't feel a thing!'

She'd dreamed of this moment, dreamed of walking down the corridor, perfectly made up, smiling at her colleagues and completely in control, such a contrast to the screaming banshee Rory was bundling into a wheelchair and whizzing down the corridor.

'Morning, Ally!' Win's voice was preposterously cheerful as Ally sailed past, clutching a vomit bowl and hating Rory with venom.

'This isn't normal,' Ally said, as Rory helped her into a gown. 'It shouldn't hurt this much.'

'It's completely normal.' Rory smiled, taking her weight in his arms and holding her as she rocked through another contraction. 'You're doing wonderfully.'

'Don't patronise me,' Ally snarled, scarcely able to comprehend she'd had the gall to tell a woman to breathe through the pain, deciding there and then that no woman should advocate natural childbirth until they'd been through it themselves. 'Where's the bloody anaesthetist.'

'The *bloody* anaesthetist is here.' Ralph grinned, breezing into the room and dragging his stainless steel trolley along with him. 'You might hate me now but in a few moments I'll be your best friend.'

And he was, Ally decided as the drugs finally hit. It was like getting drunk in reverse, her mind incredibly clear while her legs tingled into numbness, the appalling pain that had gripped her so violently abating to such a degree that Rory had to tell her when she was having a contraction.

'Let's get you over to Theatre.' Jess appeared. 'Rinska's ready for you.'

'Are you sure?' Rory smiled down at Ally. 'If you want to try to have a…'

'I want this baby out,' Ally broke in, and her words were delivered so strongly she almost managed to convince herself that she meant it. But as they wheeled her past the delivery rooms she knew so well and down the corridor towards Theatre, Ally felt a pang of regret for what she was missing out on. But as Rory squeezed hard on her hand, any regrets disappeared. She focused on all she had instead of what she was missing—a Caesarean section a tiny price to pay for Rory's peace of mind, knowing how scary this moment was for him.

And if she couldn't have Rory deliver her then Rinska was her next choice. The very new consultant winked glittery blue eyelids at Ally, and told her that her baby would be there soon.

'Ready?'

And even if it wasn't the most natural of

births, surely it was the most beautiful. All the theatre staff held their breath as Rinska delivered the head. Delicious rasping cries filling the room before the rest of the body was even out. Ally had a glimpse of her son over the dark green screen as Rinska held him up.

'A boy,' Rory shouted, thumping the air as if he'd just scored a goal. 'Look at him, Ally.'

And she was looking! In fact, she was almost fainting at the sight of him. This wasn't just a big baby—he was huge! Dark blue eyes that would surely turn green in a matter of days were staring knowingly back at his mother, fat fists flailing in the warm theatre air.

'What a bruiser,' Rinska called as the nurse called out his weight.

Any lingering desire to have had a vaginal delivery rapidly faded away.

'You're amazing.' Kissing her forehead, Rory whispered those intimate words to her and she stared back at him, at a man who had endured so much just to give her this moment, who had faced his fears and conquered them. Ally knew then that she'd lied when she'd confronted him back on the beach all those months ago, lied when she'd told him she'd have moved on easily without him. Because no one could have filled Rory's shoes. She'd have waited as long as it took had she known she'd have this moment.

'I am, aren't I?' Ally smiled back, gazing at her son, scarcely able to believe that she had somehow *grown* a boy. But staring up at Rory, his huge arms wrapped tenderly around his newborn son, Ally knew there and then that she wasn't the only one who had produced something amazing today. Reaching up, she captured his hand and closed her eyes as he kissed her tenderly on her cheek. 'And so are you.'

MEDICAL ROMANCE™

Large Print

Titles for the next six months…

February

THE SICILIAN DOCTOR'S PROPOSAL	Sarah Morgan
THE FIREFIGHTER'S FIANCÉ	Kate Hardy
EMERGENCY BABY	Alison Roberts
IN HIS SPECIAL CARE	Lucy Clark
BRIDE AT BAY HOSPITAL	Meredith Webber
THE FLIGHT DOCTOR'S ENGAGEMENT	Laura Iding

March

CARING FOR HIS CHILD	Amy Andrews
THE SURGEON'S SPECIAL GIFT	Fiona McArthur
A DOCTOR BEYOND COMPARE	Melanie Milburne
RESCUED BY MARRIAGE	Dianne Drake
THE NURSE'S LONGED-FOR FAMILY	Fiona Lowe
HER BABY'S SECRET FATHER	Lynne Marshall

April

RESCUE AT CRADLE LAKE	Marion Lennox
A NIGHT TO REMEMBER	Jennifer Taylor
THE DOCTORS' NEW-FOUND FAMILY	Laura MacDonald
HER VERY SPECIAL CONSULTANT	Joanna Neil
A SURGEON, A MIDWIFE: A FAMILY	Gill Sanderson
THE ITALIAN DOCTOR'S BRIDE	Margaret McDonagh

MILLS & BOON®

Live the emotion

0107 LP 2P P1 Medical

MEDICAL ROMANCE™

Large Print

May

THE CHRISTMAS MARRIAGE RESCUE Sarah Morgan
THEIR CHRISTMAS DREAM COME TRUE Kate Hardy
A MOTHER IN THE MAKING Emily Forbes
THE DOCTOR'S CHRISTMAS PROPOSAL Laura Iding
HER MIRACLE BABY Fiona Lowe
THE DOCTOR'S LONGED-FOR BRIDE Judy Campbell

June

THE MIDWIFE'S CHRISTMAS MIRACLE Sarah Morgan
ONE NIGHT TO WED Alison Roberts
A VERY SPECIAL PROPOSAL Josie Metcalfe
THE SURGEON'S MEANT-TO-BE BRIDE Amy Andrews
A FATHER BY CHRISTMAS Meredith Webber
A MOTHER FOR HIS BABY Leah Martyn

July

THE SURGEON'S MIRACLE BABY Carol Marinelli
A CONSULTANT CLAIMS HIS BRIDE Maggie Kingsley
THE WOMAN HE'S BEEN WAITING FOR
Jennifer Taylor
THE VILLAGE DOCTOR'S MARRIAGE Abigail Gordon
IN HER BOSS'S SPECIAL CARE Melanie Milburne
THE SURGEON'S COURAGEOUS BRIDE Lucy Clark

MILLS & BOON®

Live the emotion

0107 LP 2P P2 Medical